KU-397-217

XB00 000014 5522

"We were rather rudely interrupted."

"So we were. You seem to have dried off nicely." He couldn't help glancing downward to the front of her white peasant blouse. And since he happened to be looking that way, he might as well linger just a moment to admire the expanse of creamy, glistening skin revealed above the deep neckline, the deep shadow of cleavage, the tiny mole just above her…

She cleared her throat. "Um, Jones?"

With an unapologetic grin, he lifted his eyes. "Yes?"

"You're being very bold, sir."

Her tone was teasing, not offended, so his grin only deepened when he murmured, "You know how it is with us epic adventurers."

"Sadly, yes." She injected just the right amount of world-weary resignation into her tone to make him laugh.

Damn, but it was fun to be with her. The only real fun he'd had tonight.

Dear Reader,

Weddings are always ripe settings for fiction. Weddings so often involve drama and humour, joy and stress, smiles and tears. The most minor crises are magnified, and the pressure for everything to be "perfect" can lead to tension for everyone involved. So it seemed only natural that Dr Madison Baker wonders if the immediate attraction she feels for fellow wedding party member Dr Jason D'Alessandro is unduly influenced by their surroundings, or if their chance encounter could lead to a lifetime partnership.

Before I became a full-time writer, I made my living in advertising and photography. Serving as the official photographer at three weddings quickly convinced me that I'd rather write about weddings than participate! I was all too easily caught up in that futile quest for perfection and the stress was overwhelming for me, but those experiences have fueled my imagination ever since when it came to writing wedding stories. I remembered those three weddings and many others I've attended since while dreaming up challenges for Madison and Jason to encounter during their initial weekend together.

Spending time with the Baker family was so much fun for me. I loved getting to know the three physician siblings, Meagan, Mitch and Madison, and bringing them together with their own special "someones." I hope you've enjoyed meeting them, too, and that you'll be entertained by Madison's adventures falling in love among the chaos of her best friend's extravagant wedding weekend.

Gina Wilkins

Doctors in the Wedding

GINA WILKINS

First published in Great Britain 2012
by Mills & Boon, an imprint of Harlequin (UK) Limited.
Large Print edition 2012
Harlequin (UK) Limited,
Eton House, 18-24 Paradise Road,
Richmond, Surrey TW9 1SR

© Gina Wilkins 2012

ISBN: 978 0 263 23017 8

Harlequin (UK) policy is to use papers that are natural, renewable and recyclable products and made from wood grown in sustainable forests. The logging and manufacturing process conform to the legal environmental regulations of the country of origin.

Printed and bound in Great Britain
by CPI Antony Rowe, Chippenham, Wiltshire

GINA WILKINS

is a bestselling and award-winning author who has written more than seventy novels. She credits her successful career in romance to her long, happy marriage and her three "extraordinary" children.

A lifelong resident of central Arkansas, Ms Wilkins sold her first book in 1987 and has been writing full-time since. She has appeared on the Waldenbooks, B. Dalton and *USA TODAY* bestseller lists. She is a three-time recipient of a Maggie Award for Excellence, sponsored by Georgia Romance Writers, and has won several awards from the reviewers of *RT Book Reviews.*

As always, for my family, who are always there for me and for each other. I've been so blessed.

Chapter One

A mysterious, smoky-eyed gypsy fortune-teller gazed back in surprise from the mirror's shiny surface. Madison Baker blinked and looked again, just to make sure the reflection was her own. "I don't know, BiBi. Maybe this costume is a little too much?"

"Too much what?" Bianca "BiBi" Lovato demanded, studying her longtime friend with a satisfied smile. "Too much cleavage? Too much leg? Too much sexy?"

"All of the above." Twisting slowly, Madison

eyed her reflection, wondering how the snug-fitting white peasant blouse BiBi had provided added the illusion of several inches to her average-size bustline. The very low, square-cut neckline with off-the-shoulder, short puff sleeves revealed more skin than Madison was accustomed to showing.

Her blond-highlighted hair tumbled from beneath a glittering purple head scarf to brush her bare shoulders. A burgundy corset accented with gold ribbons and threads laced tightly from just below her breasts to the top of her hips, making her waist look startlingly small above a cleverly draped purple sash. The flirty, ruffled skirt in burgundy, purple, gold and black was bunched high on her right thigh, baring her right leg almost to dangerous territory. Large hoop earrings swung from her lobes and bangle bracelets clinked with the movements of her arms. Ridiculously high heels on a pair of BiBi's barely-there gold sandals added a good five inches to

Madison's already long legs. She was glad she'd made time in her hectic schedule for a mani-pedi earlier that week.

She lifted her arms a little higher, just to make sure everything that was supposed to be covered remained that way. The bracelets clanged gaily with the movement. "I like it," she decided aloud. "It's fun."

BiBi clapped her hands. "I knew this costume would be fantastic on you. I'm so glad you let me pick one out."

"I really appreciated your offer. I've worked like a crazy person the past couple of weeks—including two nights on call at the hospital—just to clear time off for your wedding festivities. There was no way I would've had time to find a costume. Nor did I have room in my luggage to bring it if I'd found anything."

Corinna Lovato, BiBi's younger sister and the maid of honor for BiBi's upcoming nuptials, pushed lightly past Madison to claim the full-length mirror. "BiBi and I chose the outfits from our cousin's costume shop. I love mine."

Corinna did look fabulous in her alien princess garb, Madison had to admit. Sparkly gray shadow and charcoal liner made her almond-shaped dark eyes look big and mysterious against her flawless skin. False green lashes sprinkled with glitter swept her cheeks when she fluttered them. More glitter had been brushed over her cheekbones, throat and cleavage. Her dove-gray gown was floor-length, skintight and cut daringly low, cinched at the waist with an intricately detailed gold metal belt that matched the elaborate headpiece securing her dark hair. Long sleeves ended in flowing points around her hands, revealing nails polished in a gleaming jade.

"You look beautiful, Corinna."

Corinna beamed over her shoulder. "Thanks, Maddie. So do you."

"We all look gorgeous." BiBi smugly included

herself and Hannah Thatcher in the comment. BiBi wore a pink-and-red genie costume that bared her midriff and most of her cleavage, and displayed her legs through pink-chiffon harem pants. Her ebony hair was caught up in a saucy ponytail secured by a felt-and-chiffon genie's cap. Hannah, who like Madison was in Dallas to serve as a bridesmaid in BiBi's wedding, had been outfitted as a pirate wench in another low-cut peasant blouse, a short, tattered-hemmed skirt, wide leather belt and a snug faux leather weskit jingling with fake gold doubloons.

The costumes were hardly original, but no one could say they were bland, Madison thought with another glance at the mirror. She'd known when she'd given BiBi authorization to rent her a costume from BiBi's cousin's shop that the results would be…interesting.

Madison and BiBi had known each other since college, having met freshman year when they had been randomly assigned as roommates their first semester. By the second week of school, they'd been very good friends. Their complex, sometimes drama-filled but ultimately worthwhile relationship had survived four years of college in Louisiana, then they'd gone on separate paths afterward for the past seven years. Madison had attended medical school in Little Rock, Arkansas, and was now in the fourth year of her psychiatry residency program. BiBi had settled here in Dallas, Texas, to work as a physical therapist. They'd stayed in contact through phone calls, email and social-networking sites, and though they had seen each other rarely during these past busy years, their friendship continued.

Local friends of the engaged couple were hosting tonight's festivities in a hotel ballroom on this Thursday evening before the planned Sunday afternoon ceremony. Mostly friends of Carl's, BiBi had confided. A member of a wealthy Dallas family with long-standing ties to local civic and charitable organizations, Carl Burleson was an aspiring politician who cultivated contacts almost obsessively. He remained in touch with all his fraternity buddies from college and classmates from law school. He even knew where most of his graduating class from high school had settled, BiBi had added with a rucful laugh. Thc oncs who could provc uscful in the future, at least. Carl was a nice guy, and people were naturally drawn to his extroverted personality, but he made no secret of his ambitions.

The costume party tonight was the kickoff to a long weekend of planned events. Even though it was only the middle of October, BiBi's wedding was as good an excuse as any to have an early Halloween celebration, their friends had insisted. BiBi had been thrilled. She never missed an opportunity to be the guest of honor at a party, no matter what the occasion.

Corinna adjusted the top of her dress, displaying just a bit more cleavage. She looked toward her sister as she asked wistfully, "Do you think he'll even notice me tonight?"

BiBi answered immediately. "You bet he will. He's probably going to take one look at you in this sexy costume and his jaw will drop to the floor. Isn't that right, girls? How could any man not notice how gorgeous Corinna looks tonight?"

Though she had no idea who the sisters were talking about, Madison joined Hannah in assuring them that Corinna was definitely irresistible. Having an overprotective sister of her own, Madison recognized the fierce loyalty in BiBi's expression. Whoever the object of Corinna's desire happened to be, he'd better be wary of hurting BiBi's little sister.

The way Corinna sighed suggested it was already too late for that. "Yeah, right. He made it clear enough that he's not interested in me as anything other than a longtime family friend.

I know I'm just wasting my time hoping he'll change his mind, but still…"

"He's a jerk," Hannah suggested.

Corinna shook her head with a slightly sad smile. "That's the problem. He's totally not a jerk. He's so kind and compassionate and thoughtful. I could tell it hurt him almost as much as it hurt me when I finally got up the nerve to ask him out and he had to tell me he wasn't interested in me that way. I thought maybe he would see me differently after I came back to Dallas from those five years in Austin, but I guess he still just thinks of me as BiBi's little sister. There's never going to be anything between us."

"Don't give up," BiBi said. "He's not seeing anyone else right now, as far as I know—and trust me, I've asked around. Maybe he's still stinging a little from the breakup with Samantha, but that was months ago. And he's been really busy with work lately. Maybe seeing you around this weekend, looking so gorgeous and grown-up, will make him realize what he's been missing out on."

Losing interest in the conversation, Madison leaned toward the mirror to touch up her lip gloss. She had to admit she was a little tired. She felt as though she'd been running full speed ever since she'd landed at the Dallas airport a few hours earlier, and that after a very difficult month crammed full of work and fellowship interviews. As a medical resident, she was used to long, busy days, but she could feel her energy flagging. An evening of lying in bed watching TV actually sounded more tempting than a sure-to-be-rowdy costume party.

That thought took her aback—TV in bed rather than a lively costume party? She was only twenty-eight, for crying out loud.

What had happened to her? Of the three over-achieving Baker siblings, she was the most relaxed, the most determined to have a life outside of work, the one who'd always enjoyed fashion and parties and music and fun. Yet as hard as she'd worked lately, she could barely remember the last time she'd just cut loose and had a blast.

Tossing her hair, she glanced toward the door of BiBi's suite, where they had gathered to change into their costumes. BiBi's other three bridesmaids all lived in the area and planned to meet them at the party, but BiBi had thought it would be fun for those staying in the hotel to primp together. And no one was arguing with BiBi this weekend, Madison thought with a stifled smile. The bride was in full diva mode, and no one had the heart—or the courage—to thwart her wishes.

Somewhat high-strung at the best of times, BiBi was a bundle of nerves and determination as the wedding she'd been planning for more than a year drew closer. Madison had already heard of a few tense moments between the bride and her wedding planner, the caterer, a couple of hotel employees and even BiBi's long-suffering parents. As fond as Madison was of her friend, she was well aware that it would be a good idea to walk on eggshells that weekend, just to keep everything calm and comfortable.

"Well?" she asked, tucking her lip gloss into a hidden zippered pocket on her wide purple-waist sash, along with the key card to her room. "Ready to go show off how good we look?"

Corinna giggled and whirled away from the mirror, her chin lifted in determination. "Definitely."

BiBi led the charge out of the suite, leaving Madison to close the door behind them.

The minute the friends stepped into the noisy, unconventionally decorated hotel ballroom, they were swept into a welcoming crowd of costumed revelers. BiBi hadn't exaggerated about how many guests would be in attendance tonight. The room was packed, leaving only a smallish opening for a dance floor at one end near the DJ's setup. BiBi and her bridesmaids were only a few minutes late arriving, but the festivities were already well under way. The music was loud, the booze free-flowing, the food plentiful and everyone seemed in the mood to have a great time. BiBi and Corinna were immediately absorbed into the crowd of their friends.

Someone pressed a mixed drink into Madison's hand and she sipped it while surveying the creative mix of costumes in the room—at least, the ones she could see clearly. Some genius had decided that very dim lighting equaled Halloween atmosphere. Colored lights flickered around the dance area, which was still almost empty this early in the evening. The booming music required close proximity for individual conversations, blending into a cacophony of chatter and laughter.

Science fiction seemed to be the predominant theme of the evening. Na'vi, Vulcans, Jedi and assorted other recognizable sci-fi icons mingled among the more generic witches, vampires and pirates in the shadowy room. A very pregnant warrior princess waddled past, nodding to her with a smile. Hannah saw a group of friends and rushed off to speak to them, leaving Madison to fend for herself. Eyeing a nearby Borg flirting with a very busty Klingon woman, Madison chuckled as she lowered her glass after taking another swallow of the deceptively innocent-tasting brew.

"My parents would be right at home here," she remarked to no one in particular.

"Seriously? Your parents would like this party?"

Surprised that anyone had even heard her amid the commotion, she turned in response to the male voice. A tall, lean man in a leather jacket, boots, khaki shirt and pants stood just behind her. A coiled whip dangled from his leather belt. His face was shadowed by a battered fedora, but she certainly recognized the costume. "Indiana Jones, I presume?"

Reaching up to nudge his hat with his thumb, he drawled, "At your service, ma'am."

Oh, my. Turned out there was a very nice face hidden beneath the brim of that dashing fedora. Dark hair, dark eyes, olive skin, white teeth, just a hint of a dint in a strong, square jaw. Yum.

Remembering that he had asked her a question, she silently cleared her throat before explaining, "My parents met at a sci-fi convention in the '70s. My late father was an avid Trekkie, and mom still likes science fiction."

He chuckled, and she took another quick sip of her drink. He was even more attractive when he smiled. She couldn't help noticing that the right side of his mouth tilted into a hint of a dimple just at the corner of his lips.

"And what about your costume?" He lowered his dark gaze from her face to study her revealing outfit. "Are you portraying a particular character?"

She felt a funny little quiver follow the path

of his survey all the way down to her exposed leg. Taking another sip of her drink, she shook her head. "Just a generic gypsy fortune-teller."

"You're much too stunning to be described as *generic,*" he commented, his deep tone intensifying her quiver to a full-blown tingle.

"Thank you. You look quite dashing, yourself." She took another long swallow of the drink, looking up at him through her heavily darkened lashes.

"That drink looks good."

She lowered the now-empty glass. "It was. Very good."

"There are some tempting snacks on those tables across the room. Would you like to join me on a food raid, Esmeralda?"

Amused by his wording, she lifted an eyebrow. "Esmeralda?"

With a chuckle, he shrugged. "Sounds like a gypsy fortune-teller name to me."

She hesitated only a moment before setting her

glass on a tray and tucked a hand beneath the arm he offered with a flourish. "I'd be delighted to accompany you on a food raid, Dr. Jones."

"Maybe after we eat, you can read my fortune in the champagne glass."

A little giggle escaped her. "That's tea leaves. I don't think they're serving tea tonight."

"Then you can read my palm."

She rather liked the image of cradling his hand in hers. "Maybe I will."

His arm flexed a little beneath her fingers, and she felt the strength there. Obviously this man stayed in very good physical condition. He carried himself with an athlete's grace befitting his choice of costume.

She supposed they should get around to introducing themselves eventually. But at the moment, it was so much fun pretending he was a globe-trotting archeologist and she a mysterious gypsy. Threading their way through the milling partygoers, they approached the tables.

He nodded familiarly to several of the people they passed, a few of whom did visible double takes upon recognizing him. Either they hadn't expected to see him there, or this was not the costume they would have predicted from him.

"Dude. Looking sharp," someone said, tipping her off that the latter guess was likely correct.

"So, Jones—see anything that looks good?" she asked, studying the almost-dizzying array of sweets and treats on the snacks tables.

"As a matter of fact, I do." He wasn't looking at the food.

She savored the little ripple of sensual awareness that coursed down her spine in response to his tilted smile. It had definitely been too long since she'd spent an evening flirting with a charming stranger.

A colorful selection of more mixed drinks was displayed nearby. She plucked a tall, thin glass from the table and tasted the clear liquid appreciatively. "Mmm. Good. You should try this."

He reached out to take the drink from her, holding her gaze with his when he lifted the glass to sip from exactly where her lips had just touched. "You're right. That is good."

The ripple of awareness turned into a tsunami. She snatched the glass back from him. He reached for a drink of his own. Their backs to the rest of the party, they stood close together while they filled their snack plates. It was necessary to stand that close, just so they could hear each other over the music.

Right.

She laughed when he slipped a pecan tart onto her already-full plate. "No more," she insisted. "I can't eat all of this."

He eyed his own equally full plate with satisfaction. "I'm going to make a valiant effort."

Turning away from the table, which was becoming crowded as other guests followed their example in helping themselves to the food, he peered into shadowy corners where seating had been arranged. "Where shall we take these?"

He was making the assumption that she would be eating with him. Fair enough. "Wherever we can find an empty space, I suppose. Not too close to the speakers, though. That music is really loud."

"Werewolves of London" was the current selection, and every wailed "aaahoo" made her eardrums vibrate. She wished someone would turn down the volume a bit. And then she winced, deciding she was sounding old and stodgy again. She renewed her earlier vow to abandon herself to the party tonight. Starting with sharing decadent snacks with a handsome adventurer.

If he found her comment off-putting, he didn't let it show, to her relief. "I have an idea. Follow me."

Happily, she thought, staying close behind him as he wound his way through the costumed revelers. She didn't even hesitate when he slipped through a set of French doors that led out to a cobblestoned courtyard.

Beautifully landscaped and discreetly lighted, the courtyard was small and quiet, fenced with wrought-iron. There were no tables, but several iron benches lined the sides. A pretty little fountain in the center of the circular garden added the soothing sound of splashing water to the tableau. Madison was a little surprised that they were the only ones outside on this nice autumn evening. October had been accompanied by very warm temperatures in Dallas this year, and while the air had cooled with sunset, she was comfortable even in her off-the-shoulder blouse. She supposed it was still early enough in the party that the others weren't yet ready to escape; or maybe no one had yet spotted the doors hidden among the over-the-top decorations.

Her companion nodded in satisfaction. "We

can eat in peace here, if you don't mind balancing your plate on your knees."

"I don't mind at all."

"Maybe you can tell my fortune while we eat?"

So they were still in character. Fun. She glanced at his coiled whip. "Only if you promise to protect me if any evildoers try to attack."

"It's a deal."

She chuckled and sank onto one of the benches, setting her drink on the wide arm. He sat beside her, leaving sufficient room between them that she didn't feel uncomfortable but close enough to be companionable. She popped a shrimp puff into her mouth and sighed in satisfaction.

He dabbed at his mouth with a black paper napkin. "Good food. I had a sandwich for lunch—I think. It was so long ago, I hardly remember."

She smiled. "Digging up mysterious artifacts keeps you that busy?"

"You have no idea."

She wasn't in any hurry to discuss work, neither her own nor whatever his job might be. That would only lead to talk about other everyday topics that would bring an end to this diverting charade. Of course she was curious about this man's real name, what he did, how he knew BiBi and Carl—but she was content to savor the passing moments until they got around to that point.

"Did you get one of these chocolate-dipped apricots?" he asked.

She glanced at her plate. "No, I don't think so."

He held an apricot to her lips. "You should taste it. Really good."

Her gaze locking with his, she took a bite.

The noise from the party drifted through the glass doors behind them, seeping into the quiet of the courtyard. A cool breeze toyed with her hair and brushed her cheek like a faint caress. Overhead, a misty gray cloud drifted across the face of the silver moon, adding to the fantasy feel of this beguiling encounter.

"Good?" he asked, his voice low, deep.

"Mmm." She licked a spot of chocolate from her lower lip. "Very good."

"You missed a spot." Still looking into her eyes, he touched his fingertip to the corner of her mouth.

Feeling that contact all the way to her bone marrow, she lifted her eyebrows and spoke lightly. "I think you are flirting with me, Dr. Jones."

His soft laughter was as rich and delicious as the chocolate. "I don't believe it takes a crystal ball to see that, lovely Esmeralda. And my name is Jason, by the way."

So she knew his real name now—at least part of it. And it didn't affect the magic at all, she realized. "I'm Madison."

He grinned as though acknowledging how amusing it was that they'd waited this long to get around to swapping first names. "Delighted to meet you, Madison."

Her gold bracelets jingled when she set her almost-empty plate aside and lifted her drink to her lips again, watching him over the rim of her glass. She supposed she should get back to the party—she hadn't participated at all, actually, and BiBi would surely wonder where she was—but how often did a girl get to sit in the moonlight with a fantasy hero?

"Speaking of crystal balls—" he set his own plate and glass aside "—you were going to read my palm after we ate?"

Looking up at him through her lashes, she drew a fingertip slowly down the center of his outstretched hand. "I see danger and adventure in your future, Dr. Jones."

His lips twitched as though she'd said something wryly amusing. "Do you, now?"

"Absolutely."

"And do I survive all that danger and adventure?"

"No question," she assured him. "I can tell you

are a man who is successful at any challenge he takes on."

Actually, she thought she might be right about that, though she based the presumption more on intuition than mysticism.

Looking pleased by her words, he asked in the same light tone, "Do you foresee a dance with a captivating gypsy in my near future?"

She liked the idea of being held in those strong arms, nestled against that broad chest. "I'd be—"

But her acceptance was cut short abruptly when the French doors opened and a couple of partiers spilled out into the courtyard, laughing so loudly and freely that there was no doubt their humor was fueled at least in part by alcohol.

"Ooh, are you telling fortunes out here?" a giggly vampiress in too-little black fabric and too much red lipstick demanded of Madison. "Tell mine!"

"No, I—"

"Here, read my palm."

The woman stuck out her hand toward Madison, then stumbled a little on her stiletto heels. The chubby caped hero with her caught her before she fell, but not before she knocked Madison's glass out of her hand. Madison gasped as the cold liquid trickled down her blouse and between her breasts.

"Oops." The other woman covered her mouth with one black-nailed hand, trying not to laugh but failing. "Sorry."

Madison was already on her feet, as was her now-frowning companion. She was sure he was trying only to help when he reached out with his napkin to dab at her wet chest.

She caught his wrist, keeping him from swabbing any lower. "I'll just slip into the ladies' room and tidy up."

"Oh, uh—" As if he'd suddenly realized what he was doing, he grimaced sheepishly and drew back his hand. "Good idea. I'll clear away our dishes."

"Thank you."

"I'll find you later?" he asked as she moved toward the doors.

She sent him a look over her shoulder. "You can try."

He grinned. "I'm always up for a challenge."

Oh, wow, that grin was as dangerous as the whip hanging from his belt. She continued reluctantly toward the ballroom, resisting an impulse to fan her cheeks with one hand. Behind her, she heard the unabashed vampiress say loudly, "Come dance with me, Indiana. Old stodgy here doesn't like to dance."

"Hey!"

Leaving them to sort it out, Madison made her way through the mingling crowd toward the ladies' room.

She was just finishing her cleanup when the restroom door opened and BiBi entered. Her genie hat was askew, and she paused in front of the mirror to straighten it.

"Some dippy woman on the dance floor just about knocked me off my feet," she complained. "Waving her arms around like she was sending semaphore flag messages and calling that dancing. Didn't even bother to apologize when she lurched off the dance area and into the group I was trying to talk to."

"Let me guess—she's dressed like a vampire?"

BiBi laughed wryly and looked at Madison's drying blouse. "Yep. I don't know her, she must have come as a guest of one of Carl's associates. You've met her, I take it?"

"So to speak."

"I don't think it's blood she's been drinking tonight."

"Not unless it's ninety-proof blood," Madison agreed ruefully, dabbing one last time at her blouse before tossing the paper towel into the trash.

"So where have you been? I haven't seen you since we came down from my suite."

"Just having snacks and mingling," Madison evaded.

She wasn't quite ready to share her evening's harmless diversion with her friend. She didn't want to risk having BiBi tell her that the debonair adventurer she'd flirted with in the moonlight was really a twice-divorced used car salesman with three kids he didn't support and a reputation for running cons on gullible, overworked, romance-starved women.

She was amused by her own overwrought imagination. From hero to pig, she thought with a shake of her head. She imagined reality was somewhere in between. But for now, she'd like to keep the hero fantasy alive. Just for a little while longer.

"Have you been having fun?" she asked to take the attention away from her own activities.

BiBi beamed. "Oh, yes. Carl looks so handsome in his astronaut uniform—have you seen him yet?"

"Yes. He looks great. Did you choose his costume, too?"

"Of course. Everyone's been toasting us, and telling us how great we look and how much they look forward to all the wedding festivities. I have to admit, I'm digging this bride thing. You probably aren't surprised to hear that I'm loving the attention."

Laughing, Madison shook her head. "Not at all surprised. But I'm delighted for you, Beebs. You deserve all the happiness you and Carl will have together."

"Aw, thanks, Maddie."

"So, what about Corinna? Has the alien princess captured her reluctant prince's heart this evening?"

BiBi's dreamy smile dipped into a scowl. "We haven't even seen him tonight. I guess he decided not to come, or he got tied up at work or something. I thought he said he was staying here at the hotel to avoid having to commute back

and forth from his condo on the other side of
Dallas, but maybe he changed his mind, or isn't
checking in until tomorrow. Corinna's disappointed, even if she is getting plenty of attention
from other guys, and even though she's pretty
sure nothing's going to happen, anyway. Maybe
instead of encouraging her, I should be advising
her to give up and try to find someone else. I
worry that she's going to get her heart broken."

"I hate to say this, but it sounds to me as if he's
just not that into her. I mean, that's what he told
her, right?"

BiBi sighed. "Yeah. But this weekend could be
the perfect chance for him to change his mind
if he and Corinna spend some quality time together, you know?"

"I think it's very sweet that you're looking
out for your sister," Madison answered diplo-
matically. "I also think you're seeing the world
through very romantic eyes right now, under-
standably so."

"Maybe you're right. As a matter of fact," BiBi added with a giggle, "there's someone I want you to meet. I think he's just your type. I can't wait to introduce you."

Wouldn't it be interesting if the man BiBi had in mind was dressed as Indiana Jones tonight? Because, talk about her type…

"His name is Allen," BiBi added with a toss of her ponytail.

Madison told herself she wasn't disappointed. Of all the men in attendance at tonight's party, what were the odds that Jason would have been the match BiBi had chosen for her?

Three women in colorful costumes swept into the restroom before Madison could politely assert that she wasn't looking for a fix-up while she was in town. Descending on the stalls and mirrors, the newcomers greeted BiBi, who introduced them all to Madison. Their conversation effectively at an end, Madison and BiBi then headed back to the party.

Madison scanned for a battered fedora as soon as she entered the raucous ballroom. A squarely built soldier in a red coat, ruffled shirt, khaki breeches and a white, ponytailed wig stepped into her path, blocking her view. He studied her with bright blue eyes as he asked BiBi, "Who is this lovely lady with you this evening, Lady BiBi? Can you wrinkle your genie nose and convince her to give me a dance?"

Laughing at his foolishness, BiBi slapped the man's arm playfully. "Allen, you're so silly. We were just talking about you. Maddie, this is Carl's cousin, Allen Burleson. Allen, this is Dr. Madison Baker, one of my dearest friends since college."

Sweeping his tricorn hat into a deep bow, Allen grinned up at Madison. "Delighted to meet you. May I have the pleasure of this dance?"

Calling on the manners her mother had drilled into her from birth, Madison smiled brightly and gave him her full attention, rather than continuing to search the room as she was tempted to do. "Of course."

The music was still fast and frantic, another novelty Halloween pop tune, but easy enough to dance to. Madison figured she could make a decent showing even in the ridiculously high heels BiBi had lent her.

"You're dressed as a fortune-teller tonight, aren't you?" Allen asked as he escorted her to the center of the dance floor.

"Yes. And you're a British soldier. A redcoat."

"That I am, my lady." He chuckled and fixed his tricorn on his head, skewing the wig just a little. Managing not to wince at his very bad British accent, Madison thought wistfully of a weathered, wide-brimmed hat, resisting a renewed impulse to take just a quick peek around the room.

"So what's your prediction for me?" he asked, leaning toward her to be heard over the music, his body beginning to jerk in a rather awkward man-dance.

Smiling, she swayed in time to the rhythm, eyeing his uniform meaningfully. "You're going to lose."

Allen heaved a heavy sigh. "The story of my life," he said, mock mournfully.

He seemed very pleasant. Nice-looking, too. But her pulse didn't race with his smiles, nor did she get weak-kneed at the thought of dancing closely to him. Maybe it was because of their more traditional introduction. Maybe had she met Jason the same way, he'd have seemed no more mysterious and fascinating to her than Allen. But then she pictured his gleaming eyes and flashing smile.

Okay, maybe not. Maybe Jason was every bit as compelling as he'd seemed.

Jason D'Alessandro felt as though he had two choices. He could head for the door and slip out of the party early, or hang around a little while longer in hopes of running into the fascinating gypsy again. He'd been pretty much pounced upon by Carl and his other friends the minute he'd walked back into the ballroom after eating, and he hadn't been able to make a graceful escape since.

Across the room, Corinna caught his eye, smiled weakly, then turned away to continue a highly animated conversation with a woman dressed in a leopard-print catsuit. He sighed. That situation was truly awkward. He was fond of Corinna, but that was all there was to it. He couldn't foresee his feelings ever developing into more, as he had made it clear to her in as tactful and considerate a manner as possible a couple of weeks ago. That conversation had surely been as painful for him as it had for her, and he still fretted about whether he'd chosen the right words. He just hoped she would finally accept the facts without being hurt—and without putting a wedge between two families who'd been connected for much longer than either of them had been alive.

He was tired. The booming music, mostly novelty Halloween tunes, was starting to give him a headache. At thirty, he was approximately the same age as the other party guests, but he was beginning to think he was too old for keg-and-costume parties.

It was rather a relief when the volume decreased and the music became background rather than prominent. A microphone reverberated, causing everyone around him to grimace and cover their ears. Someone laughed into it, and then a round of somewhat intoxicated toasts toward BiBi and Carl began. It sounded as though they could go on for a while.

Remembering that pleasant interlude in the courtyard earlier, he snagged another cocktail and slipped through the doors while everyone else was laughing at the string of suggestive jokes coming from the microphone. He'd take just a few quiet minutes, he promised himself, then he'd return to the party. Or maybe he'd come up with an excuse and leave for the night.

When he saw the beautiful gypsy standing in the courtyard, sipping champagne and gazing meditatively at the fountain, he decided maybe he'd stay awhile longer, after all.

The embedded lights in the garden played softly across Madison's features, glittered from the gold accents of her colorful costume and reflected in her blue eyes when she looked up at him. Moonlight bathed her bare shoulders and silvered the soft waves of blond hair spilling from beneath her headscarf.

"Hello again, Dr. Jones."

Chapter Two

Jason got a kick out of hearing Madison call him that whimsical nickname in her sultry, musical voice. Though he wasn't usually a man who indulged in fantasy, he found it easy to slide right into the character of suave adventurer with her. "You don't seem surprised to see me, Esmeralda."

She smiled up at him from beneath her thick lashes when she took another taste of her champagne. "I *am* a fortune-teller," she reminded him with a soft jingle of bracelets as she indicated

her very flattering—and delightfully revealing—outfit.

"You never got around to telling mine earlier."

"We were rather rudely interrupted."

"So we were. You seem to have dried off
nicely." He couldn't help glancing downward to
the front of her white peasant blouse. And since
he happened to be looking that way, he might as
well linger just a moment to admire the expanse
of creamy, glistening skin revealed above the
low neckline, the deep shadow of cleavage, the
tiny mole just above her...

She cleared her throat. "Um, Jones?"

With an unapologetic grin, he lifted his eyes.
"Yes?"

"You're being very bold, sir."

Her tone was teasing, not offended, so his grin
only deepened when he murmured, "You know
how it is with us epic adventurers."

"Sadly, yes." She injected just the right amount
of world-weary resignation into her tone to make

him laugh. Damn, but it was fun to be with her. The only real fun he'd had tonight.

He motioned toward the open French doors, through which they could still hear voices, laughter and music. "You're missing the toasts."

She glanced that way, then lifted one shoulder in a slight shrug. "There will be plenty more this weekend. I needed a little break."

"Yeah. Me, too. With all those people in there, it gets too stuffy inside."

She nodded. "It is warm in there. It's very nice out here."

"Yes, it is." He made it clear he wasn't talking now about the temperature.

She smiled at him again. She had a very nice mouth. Beautifully curved, the lower lip full and soft-looking, gleaming with a subtle gloss that made him want just a little taste—though he suspected he wouldn't be content to stop with a mere nibble.

The noise level behind him had abated somewhat. Music began to play, suggesting the dancing was starting up again. In contrast to the faster tunes of before, this number was slower, more relaxing. Maybe everyone else was getting a little tired, too, he thought with a faint smile.

Madison tilted her head in recognition of the tune. "'Bewitched, Bothered and Bewildered,'" she murmured. "I love this song."

The title summed up quite well the way he felt at that moment. It was unlike him to get so carried away.

"Let's not waste the song," he said, holding out his arm to escort her inside. "We still haven't had our dance."

She tucked her hand beneath his elbow, smiling up at him. Covering her hand with his, he didn't immediately move toward the doors. His gaze lingered on her glistening lips.

Her brows rose. "Was there something else?"

"I was just thinking—any movie hero worth

his salt would be unable to resist stealing a kiss in the moonlight from a beautiful gypsy."

Her smile wavered, but he wouldn't say she looked displeased by his impulsive comment. He was surprised the words had escaped him, to be quite honest. Something about this night, this party, this costumed encounter—or maybe something about this woman—brought out a flirtatiously playful side of him even he rarely saw. Especially lately, when he'd been so swamped with obligations and responsibilities that there had been little time for play.

If he were to make a guess, he would say Madison was as tempted as he to take advantage of that private moment. Her gaze held his, and he was certain he saw an answering spark of recklessness ignite in her deep blue eyes.

"Since we'll only be a movie hero and a gypsy for a little while longer, maybe we shouldn't waste the moonlight," she said, confirming his suspicion.

His pulse rate kicked into a higher gear even as he grinned in response to her tone. Flirty. Fun.

In that same spirit, he pushed his fedora back on his head and touched his lips to hers. She tasted as sweet as he had predicted. He felt a jolt of hunger when her mouth moved softly beneath his.

He had intended to keep it casual. Just an innocuous brush of lips, a champagne-flavored impulse that would make them both smile when they remembered it later. Instead, he found himself lingering. The light touch became a firm press of mouth to mouth. Her lips parted, moist and inviting, and it would have taken a much stronger man than he to resist the opportunity to explore more deeply. His tongue dipped, hers welcomed, the teasing underscored by a smoldering heat that threatened to flare into something much more serious.

He slid a hand down her back, feeling the soft warmth of her through the thin gypsy blouse.

He forced his hand to rest at the curve of her hip, though he would have liked very much to allow it to explore at will. As she had pointed out, this diverting charade would come to an end soon. He wouldn't want to do anything either of them would regret tomorrow. With that thought, he started to lift his head, ordering himself to bring the kiss to an end much sooner than he would have liked.

She wrapped a hand around the lapel of his leather jacket and drew him back to her, making it clear that she was no more satisfied by that fleeting contact than he was. More than happy to satisfy her curiosity—not to mention his own— he covered her mouth with his again, making no pretense at playfulness now.

Madison blamed it on the moonlight. Maybe the champagne. Or maybe it was the enticing fantasy of kissing a dashing stranger in a se- cluded garden while one of her favorite songs drifted through the cool air surrounding them. Only a few feet away, dozens of noisy revelers danced, laughed, drank and ate, oblivious to the intimate tableau in the cozy courtyard.

How could she possibly have resisted taking advantage of this stolen moment?

Jason could definitely kiss. His lips were firm, warm, skilled. The kisses were thorough, but not presumptuous enough to make her in any way uncomfortable. Though he held her closely, sending a thrill of awareness all the way to her toes, she knew she could step back at any moment and he wouldn't try to stop her. There was just enough restraint in his embrace that she understood he was leaving the progression to her.

She really should end it soon, but it was so nice to drift just a little longer in the illusion. She allowed her arms to slide around his neck, her fingers dipping into the thick, dark hair beneath his fedora. Her actions brought them even closer together, upthrust breasts pressed to muscular chest. She felt her insides go warm and liquid.

It took her a moment to notice the vibration between them, and then a heartbeat longer to acknowledge it wasn't the embrace causing the sensation. When she realized Jason's cell phone was demanding his attention from a pocket in his jacket, she reluctantly conceded that reality was insistently reasserting itself. With a slight sigh, she lowered her arms and took a step backward. Her high heels wobbled just a little on the bricks underneath her feet, but she kept her balance despite the weakness in her knees.

"Maybe you should answer that," she suggested, keeping her tone even and breezy, as if kissing strangers was something she did on a regular basis. "It could be important."

"They're all important," he muttered, his voice a little gravelly. He glanced at the phone, then shook his head. "It'll wait. How about that dance?"

"I'd like that." She walked beside him into the hotel, thinking that a slow dance would be the perfect way to end this unexpectedly enchanted evening. She would bet Jason danced as skillfully as he kissed. And she already knew exactly how good it felt to be wrapped in those strong arms. Heavenly.

The ballroom lights had been dimmed even more while they were outside, maybe to suit the more restrained and romantic music now drifting from the speakers. The dance floor was crowded with costumed hobgoblins and heroes pairing up as the party wound down for the night.

She'd been right when she'd predicted that Jason would be a good dancer. He was. And she further suspected that he would be very good at many other things. Unbidden images swirled slowly in her head, making her pulse flutter in her throat. There was a limit to how reckless she was willing to be tonight—but it didn't hurt to fantasize a little while she swayed in Jason's arms.

He smiled down at her. "This is nice."

"Yes."

"Are you going to the ranch thing tomorrow?"

She nodded. "That's the plan."

Thinking of how early BiBi expected everyone to turn out for the planned day at a local dude ranch, she glanced around at the still-partying crowd, wondering wryly how many would show up with bloodshot eyes and pounding heads. Considering how little sleep she'd had lately, she should probably turn in soon, herself, if she was going to get into the spirit of BiBi's cowboy celebration.

"You'll be there?" she asked, telling herself that would be as good an incentive as any to get her out of bed early.

"That's the plan." He chuckled as he quoted her.

To her regret, the song ended and she moved

reluctantly out of his arms. Almost immediately, BiBi appeared at her side. Though BiBi smiled broadly, Madison knew her friend well enough to sense that she was displeased. Was BiBi annoyed that Madison was dancing with someone other than Allen, whom BiBi had decided was the ideal weekend match for Madison?

"Maddie," BiBi said a bit too brightly, "Allen was looking for you. I think he wants another dance. And Jason, Carl was just asking about you. He wants to make a few more arrangements with all the groomsmen. He's over there by the bar."

"I'll catch up with him in a few minutes," Jason promised. "I was just—"

BiBi slipped her hand under Jason's arm, giving a tug that looked gentle, but Madison suspected was quite firm. "I'll take you over to him. I know he wanted to make sure he talked to you all tonight. Maddie, I think I saw Allen over by the desserts table."

BiBi could not have been more transparent in separating Madison and Jason. It seemed a little odd to Madison—why was her friend so intent on setting her up with the groom's cousin? Jason looked over his shoulder as BiBi towed him away, giving Madison a smile of resignation and mouthing the word *later*.

It wouldn't be later tonight, Madison decided abruptly. She was really tired. Certainly not in the mood to dance again with Cousin Allen, not even to keep BiBi happy. Spotting Hannah standing near the exit, she headed that way. She explained to Hannah that she was really tired, having been post-call yesterday and traveling today. She was going to get some rest and be fresh for tomorrow's early plans. Sympathetically, Hannah promised to relay the message to BiBi, wishing Madison a good night's sleep.

It wasn't rude that she hadn't said good-night to Jason, Madison assured herself as she made her way toward the ballroom exits. It was simply in character for the role she had played tonight. A mysterious gypsy fortune-teller would fade into the shadows without a goodbye, right? The footloose adventurer he portrayed would expect nothing more.

And besides, she thought with a ripple of anticipation, she would see him again tomorrow. She couldn't wait to find out if he looked as good on horseback as he did on the dance floor. She suspected he would.

The first thing she did after closing herself into her hotel room was to kick off the stiletto sandals and let her poor, aching feet sink gratefully into the carpet. She yanked off the headscarf and threw it onto a chair, pushing a hand through her hair. The purple waist sash went next. Little by little, she was transforming back into herself.

Stripping down to her panties and strapless bra, she tossed the costume over the back of the chair and reached for a nightgown, replaying the evening's events in her mind. She fancied that her lips still tingled a little from the impetuous kisses, and it was a nice feeling she wanted to hold on to for a while longer. Not that she expected anything serious to come of the flirtation, even if she spent time with Jason again tomorrow at the dude ranch.

Tonight had all been in fun, just a little extra entertainment at the costume party. Yes, he'd been charming and amusing and so darned sexy her toes had curled when he'd smiled at her. She'd been disappointed when BiBi had carried him off, but she hadn't intended to take their encounter any further tonight; as much as she enjoyed flirting, it wasn't her style to hook up with strangers.

Tossing the strapless bra onto the chair with the abandoned gypsy garments, she hummed beneath her breath, "Bewitched, Bothered and Bewildered." Every time she heard that song in the future, she would think of stolen kisses with a sexy stranger. And she was quite sure she would smile in response to the lovely memories.

Tired to her toenails, she crawled into bed a short while later, her teeth brushed, her face scrubbed clean of the sultry makeup, all traces of the gypsy fortune-teller gone now. And if she dreamed of kissing a dashing adventurer in the silvery moonlight—well, that would just be the ideal way to complete a near-perfect evening.

Jason was not particularly surprised to find that Carl's brief message for him could have waited until later. Nor when BiBi just happened to bring Corinna over to join them before Jason could wander off in search of Madison again.

BiBi wasn't the only one in the Lovato or D'Alessandro families who had recently decided that Jason and Corinna made a lovely couple. He had lost count of how many pointed hints had been aimed at him from all sides since Corinna had moved back to Dallas after completing pharmacy school in Austin. Even his elderly paternal grandfather had declared that Jason should ask the girl out. She was pretty, she was smart and she was the granddaughter of Vinnie D'Alessandro's lifelong friend Savio Lovato. Vinnie had been hoping to see a match between his family and Savio's for the past two generations.

Vinnie was just going to have to keep hoping, Jason thought with a slight shake of his head.

He wondered how much Corinna had been influenced by that family manipulation. Though they had been acquainted since childhood, he was six years her senior and they hadn't spent much time together, actually. She didn't even know him on a truly personal basis. Whatever her idea of who he was and what he wanted for the future, he would bet she was mistaken for the most part.

He refused to be nudged and prodded into a relationship with a woman just to please their families. If or when he chose to get seriously involved with anyone—something that hadn't tempted him since he'd broken up with his last serious girlfriend almost a year ago—he wanted it to be entirely his choice, and based on more than a comfortable acquaintance. He wanted sparks. Sizzle. Magic, he thought, startled by his uncharacteristic musings.

Even as he told himself he was being ridiculously romantic, he found his mind filled with the image of a pretty blond gypsy. Their moonlight kisses had definitely sparked and sizzled. He fancied he could taste her on his lips. It wouldn't have been hard to convince himself that she did, indeed, have magical powers.

But maybe that was the liquor speaking, he told himself with another shake of his head, setting down the glass someone had just handed him.

"A new song is starting," BiBi exclaimed with obviously feigned innocence. "Carl, we should dance at least one more time before we call it a night. Jason, have you had a chance to dance with Corinna tonight?"

He had just opened his mouth to say his good-nights, but BiBi had put him on the spot now. He didn't blame Corinna; there was no mistaking the chagrin in the look she gave BiBi. But because so many people were waiting for his response, he smiled blandly and held out a hand. "Of course. May I have this dance, Corinna?"

She nodded and accompanied him to the dance floor, which was beginning to thin a bit as the hour grew later. "That Old Black Magic" was just beginning to play from the speakers. Great, Jason thought with a sigh. A slow song. Why couldn't it have been "The Monster Mash?"

Corinna gazed up at him from beneath her long, sparkly green lashes. "I'm sorry. I didn't know BiBi was going to order you to dance with me. This must be very awkward for you."

"Not at all," he assured her, lying through his teeth. "Have you had a good time tonight?"

She tossed her head a bit. "I've had a great time," she said a bit too enthusiastically. "I've danced so much my feet are numb. And I've met some very nice people. Friends of Carl's, mostly."

Male friends, she might as well have added. He hoped all her new friends were as nice as she'd said. And that she would fall head over heels in love with one of them, and have her feelings returned.

He still refused to believe Corinna had strong, serious feelings for him—again, she just hadn't spent enough time with him for that to develop—but maybe she had a little crush. After all, he was somewhat older, and a doctor, which some people found impressive, and their families had probably made him sound like a real catch to her. He supposed he should be flattered, but it was inopportune, especially this weekend with so much of the family milling around watching them. And when he'd already met someone else he would like to spend more time with during the next few days, without worrying about Corinna and BiBi glaring at him every time they spotted him with Madison.

The music ended. He dropped his arms in secret relief and took a step backward. "Your sister has a lot of activities planned for the rest of the weekend. Sounds like she's going to keep everyone busy until the ceremony."

Corinna nodded, her expression shuttered. "You'll be at the ranch tomorrow?"

"Are you kidding? BiBi would track me down if I didn't show up. I've got someone covering for me at the clinic this weekend, so I'm free to do my duties as a groomsman, whatever that entails."

He was very glad Carl had asked his brother, Curtis, to serve as best man. With Corinna serving as maid of honor, she and Curtis would be the ones walking together during the ceremony. Jason wasn't sure who he'd be paired with for the ceremony, but he was relieved that he wouldn't be escorting Corinna down the aisle and making the older family members sigh wistfully at the symbolism.

Now if only she'd tell her older sister to back off.

He hoped it wouldn't be too uncomfortable for him to spend more time with Madison tomorrow. One way or another, he was definitely going to try.

Accustomed to getting up early for work, Madison was wide awake at six-thirty Friday morning. As tired as she'd been the night before, she was rather surprised to wake fully recharged and ready to go.

The vans to the dude ranch were scheduled to leave at nine. Judging from how quiet the halls were outside her room, she would bet most of the other wedding guests were sleeping off last night's party, perhaps planning room service breakfasts before gathering in the lobby as BiBi had instructed. A breakfast buffet was served downstairs for hotel guests, but Madison wasn't hungry yet. She was in the habit of going for an early run before breakfast.

A quick check of hotel amenities let her know a gym was available for guests, along with two indoor pools—one for swimming laps, the other designed for family use. Deciding she'd swim a few laps in lieu of her run, she donned the simple black suit she'd brought with her, covered it with a T-shirt and yoga pants and slid her feet into sandals. Pulling her honey-blond hair into a loose ponytail, she tucked her key card into her smartphone case and carried it with her as she headed for the elevator.

Waiting for the car to arrive, she found her thoughts drifting to the man she had met last night, and whom she would be seeing again on today's outing to the ranch. Jason had been devastatingly handsome in his dashing costume, but she'd bet he looked just as delicious in jeans and boots. She was definitely looking forward to finding out.

Thinking of spending more time with him filled her with such anticipation that she couldn't help feeling a bit like a giddy schoolgirl. It was a nice feeling, she decided, one she hadn't felt in much too long. She was long overdue for a fun flirtation. It was good for her to stay in practice, she thought with a quiet laugh.

Because it was so early, she encountered only a few industrious souls heading for the workout room. The lap pool was across the hall from the gym. She pushed open the glass doors and stepped into the humid warmth. Surrounded by gleaming tiles and inviting chairs, the big pool dominated the solarium-styled room. The scent of chlorine tickled her nose. Glass walls overlooked the parklike grounds of the hotel.

Glass panes above revealed the pale blue, early-morning sky of an autumn day that promised to be clear and comfortably temperate.

Only one other person was in the pool, a man swimming laps with strong, steady strokes designed more for fitness than fun. He stayed on one side of the long pool, so she didn't think there would be any problem with her swimming on the other side. She kicked off her sandals and pulled her T-shirt over her head. Her functional black one-piece was form-fitting, but modest enough that it didn't bother her to strip out of her yoga pants in preparation for her swim. Maybe the other swimmer would finish soon and she'd have the pool to herself for a while.

Someday, once she settled somewhere to begin her practice, she would have a house with a pool and these early-morning laps would be commonplace for her. She had always enjoyed a good swim.

She stepped onto the pool steps and descended

into the waist-deep water. Noticing her, the man completed a lap, pushing a hand through his dark, wet hair as he dropped his feet to the bottom of the pool and stood, beads of water glistening on a beautifully sculpted expanse of chest. She took just a microsecond to admire that attribute before she glanced surreptitiously at his face—and then froze in surprise.

"Jones?"

Chapter Three

The nickname had escaped before she could replace it with his real name, illustrating she still
thought of Jason as the fantasy man from last
night. She should probably work on that or risk
disappointment. Reality couldn't possibly be as
ideal as last night had been—though she had to
admit he looked pretty darned perfect standing
there all wet and sleek.

He whipped his head around, then broke into
a grin. "Esmeralda. Good morning."

Oh, heavens, did Jason look good naked! Okay,

he wasn't really naked, considering he wore a pair of dark swim trunks, but near enough that her overactive imagination had little trouble filling in the blanks. The pool water was kept at a comfortable temperature, but she felt overly warm as she gazed at him and tried to think of something witty and halfway coherent to say.

"Guess I'm not the only early riser," he commented, wading in her direction.

"I'm in the habit of getting up early for work," she admitted, trying to keep her eyes on his face. "Usually I go for a run to wake me up, but I thought a swim would be nice this morning."

Okay, hardly witty, but at least coherent. Although she wasn't sure she could remain so if he didn't stop looking at her that way. The open appreciation in his gaze was definitely flattering.

"I like to start the day with physical activity, myself."

She wondered if he'd intended the double entendre, or if she was getting carried away with their flirting. Deciding the latter was true in any case, she motioned toward the open expanse of pool. "I hope I'm not disturbing your swim."

He gave her one of his patented smiles. "Only for the better. Don't let me keep you from your exercise. I planned to swim a few more laps, myself."

His grin triggered a renewal of their playfulness from last night. Mischief crowded out self-consciousness as she swept a hand through the water and asked in quiet challenge, "Think you can keep up with me?"

Something flared in his dark eyes as he waded a step closer to her. "I'd certainly like to try."

"I've been told I'm hard to catch." She reached out to brush a drop of water from his cheek, trailing her fingers along the firm edge of his jaw to the faint indention in his chin. She pressed one fingertip into that shallow hollow and imagined letting the tip of her tongue follow the path her fingers had just taken, ending with a little bite just there.…

As if reading her thoughts in her expression, he shifted closer to her. She snatched her hand away and turned to dive into the water, striking out with firm, steady strokes to begin her first lap. She heard a laugh and a splash behind her, but didn't stop to look back. She had issued a challenge, after all. And she did not like to concede defeat.

It took only half a lap for him to draw up beside her. He made no effort to surge ahead, though she conceded in resignation that he could have if he'd tried. Instead, he kept pace with her, nearby but staying out of her way. She didn't know how long he'd been swimming before she'd joined him, but he showed no signs of tiring. The man definitely had stamina. Not that she'd had any doubt he was in excellent shape. She had a very clear memory of every muscle she'd felt while pressed against him last night.

If being that close to him fully clothed had been such a memorable experience, she could only imagine what it would feel like now—wet flesh to flesh. For just a moment, her strokes fumbled, losing her rhythm so she had to make an effort to get back into sync with him.

"Okay?"

"Fine," she sputtered, and swam a little faster to relieve a sudden surge of hyper energy.

Her endurance was beginning to flag a few laps later, and Jason must have noticed. She felt a hand on her leg, a tug on her ankle. Considering the electricity she sensed between herself and Jason, she wouldn't have been surprised if the water conducted a shock when their skin made contact. Or maybe it had, explaining the tingle coursing through her body when she lowered her feet to stand and face him.

"I'd love to stay longer, but I have a few calls to make before we leave for the ranch," he said with visible regret. "Guess I'd better go take care of them."

She nodded, reminding herself she would be seeing him again soon—though it would be different when they were surrounded by other people rather than alone here together. "I should get ready, too. BiBi would strangle me if I'm late."

He chuckled. "None of us have the nerve to annoy BiBi, especially this weekend."

"Ah. So you know the bride as well as the groom," she teased.

He nodded. "I've known them both for years."

It would be tempting for her to grill BiBi later for more information about Jason, but that seemed rather impolite. Besides, BiBi would want to know all the details and would probably make more of Madison's interest than was justified, not to mention that BiBi had picked out someone else to keep Madison company this weekend. All in all, it was better—and definitely more fun—to just keep this flirtation a little secret between herself and Jason.

She turned toward the steps. "I'll see you at the ranch, then, if not before."

He caught her arm, and though he was barely touching her, she was still as affected as she'd imagined by the flesh-to-flesh contact. *Honestly, Madison, get a grip,* she scolded mentally. One would think she'd never had an instant connection with a handsome man before. Okay, maybe she hadn't experienced anything quite like this, but still, there was no need to get so carried away.

"Was there something else you wanted to say, Dr. Jones?" she asked, keeping it light.

His gaze focused on her smile. Was he, too, remembering last night's kisses in the moonlight-bathed, aromatic garden, wondering if they would be just as powerful here in this brightly lit, chlorine-scented room?

Something beeped from a small table near the end of the pool, and Jason released her arm. Madison told herself it was just as well they'd been interrupted. She could only imagine the gossip that would ensue if she were seen kissing Jason in the pool after meeting him only last night.

"That's the alarm I set on my phone to remind me of the calls I have to make."

"I'll see you later, then."

He reached out to trail a wet fingertip down her cheek. "I look forward to it," he murmured.

Her body temperature rose another few degrees. She swallowed a sigh as she watched him climb the steps out of the pool, water streaming from his lean, toned body, his trunks molded over a very tight butt.

The laughing glance he gave her over his shoulder let her know he was fully aware she was watching him. She grinned and dove back into the pool.

* * *

When she left the pool room a short time later, her limbs were pleasantly tired, and her tummy reminded her that she should have breakfast soon. The day ahead seemed especially inviting now. She'd thought the ranch excursion sounded like fun, anyway, but the anticipation of spending time there with Jason was especially appealing. She couldn't wait to see him on horseback.

Hannah stepped out of the workout room at almost the same time Madison entered the hallway. Exchanging cheery good-mornings, they moved together toward the elevator.

"Have you eaten breakfast yet?" Hannah asked.

Madison glanced at her watch. A quarter to eight. Plenty of time yet before the nine o'clock departure. "No. I'm going to shower and dress, then head down to the breakfast buffet before we leave for the ranch."

"Sounds like a plan. I'll meet you down there."

Madison pushed the call button. "I can be ready in half an hour."

"Same here." Hannah pushed back a strand of hair that had escaped her red braid during her exercise session. "I thought I saw Jason D'Alessandro leaving the pool room a little while ago. Did you meet him?"

Though this was the first time she'd heard Jason's last name, Madison nodded. "I met him at the party last night."

"I met him last night, too. BiBi introduced us. I think you were dancing with Carl's cousin at the time. Jason seems like a nice guy. Good-looking, too."

"Yes, he is."

"I can see why Corinna is so hooked on him."

Madison almost stumbled stepping into the elevator. She righted herself quickly, punching her floor button with a little more force than necessary. "Umm, Corinna?"

"Yeah. He's the guy she and BiBi were talking

about last night. Didn't you know? Apparently, Corinna's had a thing for him for ages. From what I've gathered, their families have known each other for, like, generations, and everyone thinks Jason and Corinna would be a perfect match. You know, both living here in Dallas, him being a doctor and her a pharmacist, both from big Italian families."

Madison stared hard at the numbers flashing above the elevator door. Jason was a doctor? "Hmm."

"But I don't know, watching them together last night? I'm not sure BiBi's right that he'll change his mind about Corinna. He was nice to her and all, but there didn't seem to be any chemistry between them. He treated her more like a cousin, or a kid sister, maybe."

"Hmm."

Hannah laughed self-consciously. "I shouldn't be gossiping about them. Just an observation."

The elevator bumped to a gentle stop and

Madison moved toward the opening doors in relief. "I'll meet you downstairs in half an hour, Hannah. That should give us just enough time to eat before we're supposed to join the others in the lobby."

"Okay, see you down—" The elevator doors closed behind Madison before Hannah could finish the sentence.

Moving robotically, Madison walked to her door and shoved the key into the slot. She muttered a curse beneath her breath when she realized she'd inserted the card upside down. Turning it over, she tried again, then shoved the door open.

Wouldn't you know, she thought wistfully, closing the door behind her, that the one man who'd brought out the reckless fun in her since... well, almost longer than she could remember... was the one man who was totally off-limits this weekend?

It wasn't as if she'd expected anything serious

to come of her flirtation with Jason, anyway, she assured herself, heading for the shower.

But, oh, it could have been a fun three days.

Two buses had been secured for transporting the guests to the dude ranch some twenty miles from the hotel. BiBi and Carl had invited the entire wedding party, several of their family members and a few miscellaneous others to attend, for a total of about forty people, as far as Madison could determine. BiBi insisted that the men should load into one vehicle and the women into the other—and again, no one argued with her. She was practically giddy with excitement about the entertainment she had arranged for her guests. Apparently the ranch specialized in hosting wedding parties, family and class reunions, company retreats and other such gatherings, and had offered a long list of activities for BiBi and Carl to select from.

Madison had dressed for the day in a three-quarter-sleeved, scoop-neck green T-shirt with jeans. The temperature was predicted to climb into the high seventies, and it was already too warm for a jacket, so she had tucked a thin sweater into her tote bag in case she needed it that evening. She didn't own a cowboy hat, but she'd worn a pair of brown leather boots that were vaguely Western in style. It had been a few years since she'd been on horseback; she only hoped she'd remembered enough of the basics so she didn't embarrass herself.

She'd arranged her honey-blond hair into a tidy French braid to keep it out of her face during the day's activities. Maybe she'd spent a bit more time than usual with her makeup—trying for a casual, but flattering look—but that was only because she knew BiBi's crowd wouldn't be caught dead without mascara and blusher. She certainly hadn't primped with anyone particular in mind, she assured herself sanctimoniously.

When she saw the other women, she was glad

she'd made the effort, whatever her motivation. Texas women were fussy about their hair and makeup, BiBi had always said, and that was in evidence today. Though jeans and Ts or button-up cotton shirts were the primary garments of choice, she saw a few shiny Western shirts festooned with rhinestones and appliqués, and enough new pairs of pointy-toed boots that she didn't doubt some of the guests would be limping a bit through the next day's events.

The bus seats were plush and roomy, but still rather cramped for the very pregnant woman who sat next to Madison. Madison remembered seeing her at the party last night, though they had not actually met.

"I'm Madison Baker," she said with a smile, raising her voice just enough to be heard over the excited chattering around them.

The other woman, a strawberry blonde with a face that was probably round even when she wasn't in the last stages of pregnancy and green eyes that were friendly despite the faint shadows beneath, introduced herself in return. "I'm Lila Polanski. My husband, Tommy, is an old friend of Carl's. He's serving as an usher Sunday. Are you one of the bridesmaids? Sorry, I should know that, probably, but I don't know BiBi or her friends very well."

"Yes, I'm a bridesmaid. I've known BiBi since college. Do you live here in Dallas?"

"No, Tommy grew up here, but I'm originally from Wisconsin. We moved to Houston a couple years ago for Tommy's job. We drove up for the wedding. Tommy thought a day at a dude ranch sounded kind of cheesy," she added in a stage whisper, glancing around to make sure BiBi wasn't within hearing range. "But I think it will be fun. Not that I can participate much."

She patted her protruding tummy with a mixture of pride and impatience.

Madison chuckled. "When is your baby due?"

"Next month. Our first. A boy."

"Congratulations."

"Thank you. Do you live in Dallas?"

Madison explained that she, too, had traveled for the wedding weekend, and they passed the remainder of the ride chatting congenially. Lila was a talker who tended to share a bit too much information quite freely with strangers. Madison liked her, though, and enjoyed the conversation. Madison's job never came up, and she saw no need to mention that she was a doctor. ob-gyn was not her specialty, and she wasn't prepared to answer a string of medical questions from the eager mommy-to-be. Better just to be another wedding guest, she thought.

She didn't know whose idea it had been for the men to stand around the bus door and help the women descend the steps onto the graveled ranch parking lot. It seemed to be taking the back-to-the-Old-West theme a bit too far, with the strapping cowboys offering assistance to the fragile ladies, but she told herself not to take it so seriously. Today was all in fun. Maybe she'd gotten a little too sensitive about gender issues in medical school, where there were still a few deeply ingrained biases toward male doctors, even though women made up nearly half of modern medical school classes. When two men rushed forward to assist Lila Polanski, Madison told herself that it really was sort of nice that Southern gallantry still existed, despite the old-fashioned gender implications.

A man in a well-worn brown hat, a denim shirt rolled back on the forearms, jeans and boots that were definitely not new stepped up when she moved into the bus door. He held out a hand to her, tilting his head back so she could see his face beneath the brim of his hat. Her breath caught hard.

She'd been absolutely correct earlier. Jason D'Alessandro looked damned good in Western wear.

Realizing she was holding up the women waiting behind her to get off the bus, Madison placed her hand in Jason's. It would have been rude to ignore his friendly offer of assistance, especially with other people watching. Among them, she realized, BiBi and Corinna, who stood nearby chatting with other guests, but still surreptitiously watching Jason.

She was glad the sparks that flew when her bare palm pressed against Jason's existed only in her own overactive imagination. Or was he aware of them, too? She thought she heard his breath catch when his fingers closed around hers, but maybe that, too, was just something she imagined. Reminding herself that he was off-limits, she withdrew her hand quickly, meeting just a little resistance when she pulled away, as if he had been reluctant to release her.

BiBi rushed forward, almost dragging a tall, lanky cowboy with her. The man wore neatly pressed dark jeans over tooled leather boots, a tan denim shirt with colorful floral embroidery up the front and across the back yoke, a bolo tie and a battered hat with a feathered band. Madison figured he was so stereotypically dressed that he must be an employee of the dude ranch.

BiBi proved the guess to be correct. "Everyone, this is Buck. He's our ranch host for today, so if anyone has any problems or questions, he's the man to ask. Right, Buck?"

He agreed congenially, then made a short welcoming speech outlining the activities planned for the day and urging everyone to feel free to ask any ranch employee for assistance as needed.

"And now let's all load up on the wagons," he said, indicating three large open wooden wagons, each with a driver holding the reins to a pair of sturdy-looking horses. "We're about to head back in time to a real Old West ranch experience."

Madison heard a few muted snorts from some of the men in the party—probably men who had either grown up on real ranches or had at least some familiarity with them. BiBi had insisted she knew this was basically an amusement-park version of ranch life, but she didn't care. It was going to be fun, she'd said. And fun was what her wedding weekend was all about. She'd also admitted to her girlfriends that she was looking forward to seeing her citified lawyer fiancé on horseback. Just because Carl had grown up in Dallas didn't make him a cowboy, she had added with a laugh. And since several of her wedding guests were from out of state, like Madison, BiBi wanted them to have a true Texas experience.

Once again the men stepped up to help the ladies onto the wagons. Again, it took two—her husband and another volunteer—to get Lila onto a bench. Madison privately wondered if it had been a good idea for Lila to attend this outing, but Lila seemed so genuinely excited to be here that she supposed no one had the heart to suggest she stay behind.

Out of the corner of her eye, she saw Jason

moving in her direction, but another man stepped between them. "There you are, Madison. You slipped away from the party so quickly last night that I didn't have a chance to say good-night. It's good to see you again today."

She forced a smile. "Hello, Allen. Nice to see you again, too."

Carl's cousin had dressed as enthusiastically for a ranch visit as he had for the costume party. His hat, boots, tooled-leather belt and embroidered red shirt all looked new, though his jeans looked to have had some use. "I see you're still a red shirt," she commented.

He laughed. "So I am. Last night I wore the colors of the losing army and now this. If I were appearing on an episode of *Star Trek,* I'd probably be killed off today. That's an old trope," he added in explanation. "The usually unnamed crew members who appeared in the background of the episodes wearing red shirts were always the ones killed in battle scenes."

Probably he wasn't trying to sound patronizing. Certainly he didn't know she came from a family of sci-fi nuts. She nodded and spoke lightly. "Yes, I know. Perhaps you'd better be extra careful today."

"I'll do that. Ready to climb into one of these wagons? I see a couple of empty seats on the nearest one here. Let me help you in."

She really wanted to ignore his proffered hand and climb into the wagon on her own, but BiBi stood nearby, nodding encouragement and smiling indulgently, so she sighed and conceded. No sparks flew when she took Allen's hand to step up into the conveyance. She released him immediately when she was safely aboard. As she took a seat on a bench, she saw Jason helping an older woman—Carl's aunt, Madison believed— onto another wagon, and then he, too, boarded that one while Allen slid onto the bench next to Madison.

BiBi and Carl sat across from them. Corinna

and Hannah took the next bench. The wagon jolted into motion, traversing a well-worn dirt path through woods that were already thinning a little for the approaching change of season. It was an absolutely beautiful morning, clear, nearly cloudless, with a pine-scented breeze to cool them during the bumpy ride. It was almost as if nature itself was loath to displease BiBi today.

The passengers chattered during the short trip, with BiBi cheerfully dominating the conversation in their wagon. Madison didn't mind that. BiBi deserved her time in the spotlight; besides, it kept Madison from having to constantly respond to Allen's flirting. The guy seemed nice enough, but was spreading on the Western charm a little too thick.

Funny how she hadn't minded Jason's teasing flirting while Allen's only vaguely irritated her, she mused with a slight frown. She really wished she'd learned sooner that Jason was the man Corinna was interested in. Again, it wasn't that she had expected anything to come of the flirtation, but she couldn't help but be disappointed that it was over. It had been pleasant. Fun.

She would have to find a way to make it clear to him that there would be no more stolen kisses. Maybe he'd get the message if she just kept her distance today, smiling breezily when they crossed paths, very polite and impersonal. Maybe he'd wonder why she'd stopped teasing with him so suddenly, but she doubted he would persist in pursuing her. He hardly knew her, after all. She wasn't so full of herself that she thought he'd actually fallen for her in the space of a few hours, despite their instant chemistry.

Technically, she knew he was free to flirt with whomever he wanted. From what everyone had said, including Corinna, he'd made it clear there was no commitment there, not even a chance for a future relationship. But remembering how wistful Corinna had sounded when speaking of Jason, and how fervently BiBi had wanted to secure her little sister's happiness, Madison knew she had to step out of this particular picture.

Her first loyalty was to BiBi, and indirectly to Corinna. She didn't even know Jason, really. Hadn't that been part of her attraction to him? The sexy stranger angle? Well, that part was over now, inevitably so. Time to focus on her purpose for being here, supporting her longtime friend and doing her part to make sure the wedding weekend was as idyllic as BiBi dreamed it would be. All of which came back around to keeping her distance from Jason D'Alessandro.

The wagons drew up side by side at the center of the ranch, and Madison just happened to meet Jason's gaze when she glanced that way. He smiled and her heart stuttered.

Okay, maybe it wasn't going to be as easy as she'd hoped to put him out of her mind.

Chapter Four

Jason couldn't figure out what was going on with Madison. Both last night and this morning in the pool, she'd been so open and approachable. He'd been certain the attraction between them was mutual, that she was amenable to spending time with him this weekend, getting to know each other better, even if only for these few days. But something had changed since they'd parted in the pool room. She seemed to be going out of her way not to meet his eyes, and when their gazes did clash, she looked quickly in the other direction. She returned his smiles, but only with the same pleasant courtesy she showed everyone else.

Maybe that was it, he mused as he accompanied the group to the first activity area, a large arena where three ranch employees waited to greet them. Maybe Madison was just being more discreet now that they were in a smaller group of people. That made sense. He wasn't particularly eager to be the topic of wedding gossip, himself. Having attended plenty of weddings among his cousins, friends and his one married sister, he knew how quickly wedding drama could become exaggerated.

He could be discreet. For that matter, he was always discreet. Last night had been so far out of character for him that he'd hardly recognized himself. He would bide his time until he had a chance to flirt with Madison in private again—at least he hoped he would have that chance. Or was she subtly letting him know that it had been fun while it lasted, but now it was time to end it?

His sisters had accused him of occasionally being oblivious when it came to women. They teased him about being a compulsive gentleman, polite and considerate to a fault, but often missing the feminine cues directed toward him. He wasn't a game player, tended to speak his mind clearly and directly and expected others to do the same. Subtlety, his sister Carly had pronounced, was completely lost on him.

Madison hadn't been at all subtle last night. She'd made her attraction to him clear, keeping it no secret that she enjoyed their teasing and flirting. He had appreciated her directness. If she was changing her style now, he just hoped he could follow the message.

As the guests all gathered in the arena, he positioned himself where he could watch Madison as surreptitiously as possible. He noticed with a frown that Allen Burleson had managed to attach himself to her side again. Madison chatted with Allen, but she seemed to be holding back a little, treating him the same as she did everyone else around them. Jason couldn't tell that she was particularly interested in Allen—or was that just wishful thinking on his part, hoping that the connection between himself and Madison had been unique?

Madison turned to laugh in response to something BiBi had said to her. The morning sun gleamed in her honey-blond hair and glittered from her laughing blue eyes. She sparkled, Jason thought, a little self-conscious at this latest flight into fantasy. It was as if everyone around her was just a little muted in comparison. The way he usually felt. Mr. Responsibility. Mr. Ordinary. But for those few hours with Madison, he'd felt different. More interesting just for being noticed by her.

Sheepishly, he told himself he was being ridiculous. Maybe it was best if he and Madison spent a little time apart now, before he made a complete fool out of himself in front of his longtime friends.

A pretty young cowgirl in tight jeans, an embroidered satin shirt and a Western hat and boots stepped to the middle of the arena, twirling a lariat around her as she introduced herself in a slightly exaggerated Texas drawl. "I'm Gayla. It's great to have you all here today, and we're going to make sure you have a great time, whether you grew up on a ranch or this is your first visit to one.

"Needless to say, no visit to a ranch would be complete without horses. We'll have some riding lessons first, then we'll take a trail ride during which we'll have an old-fashioned chuck wagon lunch. Those of you who choose not to get on a horse will be treated to a wagon ride," she added with a glance at Tommy Polanski's very pregnant wife, who nodded in resignation.

"Okay, then." Gayla motioned forward three

ranch employees who'd been hovering behind her. "Shane and Mickey and Laura are going to help us get started."

With practiced efficiency, Gayla and her assistants separated the guests into levels of proficiency, from those who'd never sat in a saddle before to the ones who had grown up with horses, and all the levels in between. The least experienced were mounted first to begin instruction on how to sit in the saddle, hold the reins and guide their mounts. Jason noted that the horses assigned to the greenhorns were placid and tolerant, looking more likely to fall asleep in midstride than to misbehave.

The laughter and teasing that ensued were good-natured, and Jason was pleased to see that both the ranch hands and the more experienced guests made a point to put the new riders at ease. While the newbies were having their lesson, the others were assigned mounts according to their preferences.

Jason managed to maneuver himself close enough to Madison to hear her say candidly, "I've ridden friends' horses and I've been on a few trail rides, but I wouldn't call myself an expert rider. I should probably have a horse that's fairly easy to handle."

Mickey, a grizzled, middle-aged man with a protruding tummy, nonexistent butt and bowed, stork legs nodded and motioned toward a pretty bay mare. "You should take Sweet Pea. I think the two of you will get along just fine."

Madison dimpled as she admired the horse. "Oh, I'm sure we will. She's so pretty."

"A pretty horse for a pretty rider," Allen proclaimed loudly, making the others roll their eyes at the blatant flattery.

Jason felt like doing the same, even though he grimly admitted that the very same thought had crossed his mind.

He found an ignominious satisfaction in watching Madison politely rebuff Allen's assistance in mounting the bay. Instead, after taking a moment to greet the horse with head strokes and murmured compliments, she moved to the left side and swung herself easily into the saddle. She fumbled a bit getting her other foot into the stirrup but recovered quickly, looking rather proud of herself for the easy mount. Oddly enough, Jason was proud of her, too.

"You look like you know your way around a saddle," Mickey commented, giving Jason a once-over.

"I'd better, or all those years I spent hanging around my uncle Jared's ranch were wasted," Jason replied with a chuckle.

Mickey motioned toward young Seth, pointed, then looked back at Jason while Seth led up a sturdy black gelding. "This is Pablo. He likes the trail rides as long as you keep him interested, don't just sit on his back like a lump."

Jason laughed. "I'll do my best. Hey, Pablo."

He held out his hand for sniffing, then rubbed

the horse's muzzle and forelock, speaking quietly to let Pablo get used to the sound of his voice. The horse blew out a breath, bobbed his head a few times, then nuzzled Jason's washed-soft denim shirt as if granting his approval.

Mickey nodded in satisfaction. "You'll do. Pablo don't care for posers. Won't let anyone wearing fancy new boots or a shiny fringed shirt get anywhere near him."

Mickey had spoken in a low voice obviously intended for Jason's ears only, rather than risk being overheard by one of the other guests in their new boots and shiny shirts. Jason laughed, then was surprised to hear an echoing laugh from close by. He and Mickey both whipped their heads around to see Madison astride her horse, having wandered close enough to have overheard the cowboy's dry comment.

"Uh, no offense to any of your friends, ma'am," Mickey said quickly, looking chagrined by his imprudence. Jason suspected the man had been

reprimanded a few times for being less than dip-
lomatic with the dude ranch guests.

"None taken," Madison assured him. "And
don't worry, I won't repeat what you said."

He nodded in relief. "Can I help you with
something?"

"Gayla said we should ask you for any assistance," she explained, glancing at Jason as if
apologizing for the interruption. "I think my
stirrups need to be adjusted a little."

"Yes, ma'am."

Mickey started to move toward her, then hesitated when Gayla called him from a few yards
away. "Mickey, can you give me a hand over
here?"

"Go ahead," Jason said, clutching Pablo's reins
loosely in one hand. "I'll help Madison with her
stirrups."

Trusting that Jason knew what he was doing,
Mickey nodded and loped away toward the
other side of the arena, where Gayla seemed to

be having difficulty pleasing one of the other groomsmen in selecting a mount.

Looping Pablo's reins around his arm, Jason smiled up at Madison. "Nice horse."

Madison patted Sweet Pea's neck. "Yes. She and I have already become friends."

"What's the problem with your stirrups?"

"They seem a little short to me. Of course, it's been a while since I've ridden, so maybe they're fine. I just thought…"

Her voice trailed away when he placed a hand on her leg, just below her knee. Intensely aware of that touch, himself—and unable to forget how it had felt to touch that same leg in the pool, all bare and wet and supple—he kept his gaze focused on the stirrup.

"It does seem a little short. You're longer-legged than you look. Take your foot out and I'll adjust it for you."

She obliged, making no response to his comment about her long legs. "You seem to be familiar with horses," she said instead.

He grinned up at her from beneath the brim of his hat. "If you're asking if I know how to adjust a stirrup without endangering your safety, the answer is yes."

Her lips twitched with an answering smile, just a hint of the teasing they had shared before. "That doesn't surprise me. Every fearless adventurer knows how to handle a horse."

He grimaced a little as he tugged on the leather strap to make sure the stirrup was fastened securely before moving around to the other side. Should he admit that his adventures had been limited to summers and weekends on his uncle's ranch, or continue their frivolous pretense that he was some larger-than-life movie hero? Because it was so rare that he got to be anything other than a routine-bound, responsible family physician, he opted for the latter—at least for a little while longer. "So we do."

Jason patted Sweet Pea to keep from startling her as he circled around her; even the gentlest horse would occasionally kick when surprised, he'd discovered the hard way as a kid. Pablo followed cooperatively with only a light tug on his reins. Pablo lowered his head to sample a clump of grass while Jason removed Madison's foot from the other stirrup. "Nice boots."

"Thanks. I used to have some real Western boots, but they wore out years ago and I didn't have time to replace them before this trip."

"These work fine with the narrow toe. At least you didn't wear sneakers or heels. Or worse, clogs," he said with a shake of his head. One of the other women guests had worn open-back shoes, despite the guidelines everyone had been sent for the day's activities. Though she'd pouted a bit, she would be riding in the wagon with Lila and a couple of older guests during the trail ride, since clogs were hardly safe in stirrups.

"I knew better than that. A friend of mine

from my high school days owned horses, and I went riding with her fairly often. I always loved riding."

He smiled up at her again. "So do I."

Their gazes held for a few heartbeats, and his fingers tightened spasmodically on her denim-covered calf.

"How does that feel?" he asked her.

She blinked a couple of times before saying briskly, "Oh. The stirrup. That's much better, thank you, Dr. Jones."

Amused, he let his fingers trail down the side of her leg. "You're most welcome, Madison."

He found that he liked the sound of her real name on his lips more than the teasing nick-name he'd given her before, even though he still grinned every time she called him Dr. Jones. Maybe that was because she was exciting and interesting enough on her own, whereas he required a disguise to change into someone more interesting than an ordinary family practitioner?

Her laugh was as warm and easy as the ones they had shared before, making him hope he was right that she was just being discreet in front of the other wedding guests. Surely there would be a chance sometime that day for them to have a few minutes of privacy, he thought optimistically.

"Problem with your stirrups, Maddie?" BiBi called out from atop the sorrel she had been assigned. Carl and Corinna sat in the saddles of a paint and a gray, respectively. The women, Jason noticed in amusement, looked much more at ease on horseback than Carl, who was known to have a weakness for sports cars and motorcycles.

"I can help you, Maddie," Allen Burleson offered quickly, nudging his chubby chestnut toward her. "I know how to adjust a stirrup."

"Thank you, but Jason's already fixed them for me." That quickly, Madison's manner had changed again. The smile she gave Jason was impersonal and her tone was identical to the one she had used with Allen when she said, "Thank you, Jason. That feels much better."

He nodded. "You're welcome."

He could be circumspect, he reminded himself again as he turned to swing himself into Pablo's saddle. If that was the way she wanted to play it, he was up for a little stealthy dalliance. That just made it all the more fun, all the more refreshing from his usual routine. Smiling to himself, he touched the brim of his hat in a courtly gesture to her and rode off to join a couple of his acquaintances at the other side of the arena. He would see Madison again later.

Madison was somewhat relieved that Jason rode some distance behind her during the trail ride. While it might have been nice to watch him—he really did look sexy as all get out on horseback—it would probably have been too hard to keep her attention on her own riding, and on the conversations going on around her.

The ride took them through a softly rolling pasture where the green grass was just fading into autumn tan, across a shallow, babbling creek no more than a couple inches deep and which the horses had obviously crossed dozens of times before. They went through a stand of trees filled with birds and squirrels and into a pretty clearing where the chuck wagon was setting up for the alfresco lunch. During the leisurely trek, the well-trained horses were sometimes single-file, occasionally side-by-side. The placid horses assigned to the inexperienced riders plodded docilely along the trail, intent on their destination, resisting any attempts to guide them onto a different path. The more spirited horses responded somewhat better to their riders' handling of the reins, but Madison suspected that the truly experienced riders, like Jason, quickly grew bored with the slow pace and firmly established path.

The casual noon meal was served with the efficiency of a formal banquet. Folding stools appeared from a wagon so the guests wouldn't have to sit on the ground. Two long folding tables held a variety of foods for carnivores and vegetarians alike. Madison filled her metal tray with a selection of grilled veggies and a grilled chicken breast, added a dollop of spicy mustard sauce, then carried her food and a plastic tumbler of lemonade to a cluster of stools where BiBi, Carl, Lila and Tommy were already seated. They invited her warmly to join them, and she pulled up a stool, joining their conversation about the wedding plans and the Polanski's impending parenthood.

Madison rather hoped Allen would find another place to sit. She'd just as soon eat in peace without having to respond to his constant overtures. He wasn't obnoxious or pushy, just somewhat wearisome, she thought a bit guiltily. Or was that only because she simply wasn't interested in him in that way?

Her internal radar kept track of the man who

had grabbed her attention in that way. Jason made no effort to join her for lunch, choosing instead to sit with a group of men who appeared to be telling hilarious jokes judging from the boisterous bursts of laughter coming from that direction. Mickey, the ranch employee who'd seemed to bond with Jason, joined that group and was soon adding to the noise level with his own barking laugh.

"Sounds like a party going on over there."

There was just enough wistfulness in Carl's voice to make BiBi's eyebrows rise. "Would you rather go eat with the single guys?"

"No, of course not, honey," Carl answered quickly. "I'd much rather be talking about wedding dresses and diapers here than swapping dirty jokes with that bunch of miscreants over there."

BiBi laughed, as did the others, and shook her head indulgently. "You are so full of it, Carl Burleson."

He pressed a hand to his black denim shirt, just over his heart. "Full of love for you, soon-to-be BiBi Burleson."

While Tommy groaned and Lila and Madison laughed again, BiBi was distracted by the name. "Maybe I should rethink keeping my maiden name. I've always thought I'd take my husband's name but BiBi Burleson just sounds so...so alliterative."

"I think it's a pretty name," Lila said. "I took Tommy's name, you know. It just seemed more efficient somehow for me and Tommy and our kids to all have the same last name."

Madison listened quietly while the others discussed the pros and cons of changing names, all agreeing that either choice was quite acceptable these days. Still, the guys seemed to approve their mates' decisions to swap. Madison thought of her own siblings, both of whom had married in the past couple of years. Her older sister, Meagan, who had already established a career as a general surgeon in Little Rock when she'd married Seth Llewellyn, had kept her maiden name. Jacqui Handy, the woman who'd married Madison's brother, Mitch, had chosen to take the name Baker. Both had their reasons for their choices and no one in the family had given those decisions a second thought.

Madison had never really considered what she'd do in that situation. Though she had dated during college and medical school, having a couple of relationships that were somewhat serious for a time, she'd never even come close to marriage. She'd told herself there was plenty of time for that sort of thing after she finished her training and was established in her practice.

Another burst of laughter came from the group behind her, and it was easy for her to pick out Jason's voice from the others, even though his was certainly not the loudest. That odd radar again—sensing him even when she wasn't looking his way. Why on earth was she so focused on him? It wasn't as if he were the only good-looking single guy there. It wasn't as if she were looking for a single guy at all. That wasn't why she was here this weekend.

Carl directed their attention in a different direction. "Looks like your little sister has made another conquest," he observed to BiBi. "Brandon McCafferty can't seem to take his eyes off her."

Madison glanced toward the younger couple, who had already eaten and were standing by their tethered horses, chatting animatedly. Madison didn't know Brandon, but she believed he would be serving as an usher for Sunday's ceremony. A friend of Carl's family, she thought someone had said. She didn't think Carl was exaggerating Brandon's fascination with Corinna. Nor did she blame the young man; Corinna looked great today, her glossy black hair tumbling down her back, her body slim and lithe in her jeans and boots, her pretty face painstakingly enhanced with cosmetics. It was obvious, as well, that Corinna was enjoying the attention. Madison suspected Corinna's bruised ego needed those strokes.

Rather than looking pleased that her younger sister was having a good time, BiBi frowned. "I hope she's not going to let herself get into a rebound thing," she said in a low voice meant solely for Madison. "It's so obvious that she and Jason are avoiding each other. I wouldn't want her to throw herself into another relationship just to prove something to Jason."

"Your sister is an adult, Beebs," Madison replied in that same quiet tone, their heads close together to keep their conversation private while Carl and the Polanskis talked about something else. "I think she can decide for herself who she wants to spend time with this weekend."

"She *wants* to spend time with Jason," BiBi countered. "But she's going out of her way not to make a pest of herself with him. At least he didn't bring a date to the wedding or anything like that. He's staying clear of Corinna, but he's not pushing some other woman into her face."

"Surely you gave him the option to bring a date."

"Of course I did," BiBi answered almost indignantly. "But he isn't seeing anyone right now, and I guess he decided not to bother with finding someone. Or maybe he just thought it would be kinder to Corinna not to, after their talk a couple of weeks ago. He's that kind of guy, you know, always looking out for other people's feelings. His sister Carly has always called him Saint Jason behind his back—or to his face when she's in the mood to annoy him."

"You and Corinna make him sound like a virtual paragon," Madison quipped. She couldn't help thinking how different the man BiBi described sounded from the charming rogue who had so smoothly stolen a kiss in the courtyard last night.

"Well, he's not perfect. That overactive sense of responsibility makes him sort of bossy at times. A little too certain he knows what's best, you know? And his commitment to his family and his patients makes it tough to have a relationship with him. His ex, Samantha, once said she sometimes felt like she was dating the whole D'Alessandro/Walker clans as often as his phone rang or their plans were interrupted by urgent summons for him or their weekends involved some family gathering or another."

"And Corinna is still interested?" Madison asked lightly.

BiBi shrugged. "Corinna understands close family connections and work obligations. It doesn't faze her. Much."

"Hmm."

BiBi had no trouble interpreting Madison's noncommittal murmur. "I know. Whatever she thinks about his schedule, he's still not interested in her."

It seemed like a good time to redirect the conversation. "Lunch was really good, BiBi. I think I'll have one of those oatmeal raisin cookies for dessert. Want me to get one for you?"

"Umm, Maddie?"

Something about her friend's tone made Madison's eyebrows rise. "Yes?"

"I've seen you talking to Jason a couple of times. And when he was helping you with your stirrups, you seemed pretty chatty. Corinna thought Jason was smiling a lot with you, too. He didn't, uh—I mean, you wouldn't—"

Madison sighed gustily. "Jason's a great-looking guy, but I'm not looking to hook up this weekend, remember? And even if he were, I'd consider him off-limits just because of the awkwardness."

BiBi looked relieved. "Thanks. I mean, I'd hate for us to get into another uncomfortable situation like that one with Steve Gleason."

Madison couldn't believe her friend had actually brought up that old falling-out. Honestly, it had been almost ten years since a college boy BiBi had a serious crush on had fallen for Madison instead. Madison hadn't thought she'd done anything to encourage him, but BiBi had insisted that Madison's warm, friendly manner toward Steve had been flirting. BiBi had refused to accept Madison's argument that she treated everyone pretty much the same way; and even if she did, BiBi had added, she shouldn't have been so nice to Steve, who'd taken her outgoingness as encouragement.

It had gotten so bad that BiBi and Madison couldn't even be in the same room with Steve, who'd inconveniently fallen all over Madison every time he saw her, to BiBi's dismay. Madison had actually had to drop a class they were all in rather than risk losing her friendship with BiBi, and had been forced to rebuff Steve's overtures somewhat more brusquely than she would have liked just to get him to stay away from her. Eventually her relationship with BiBi had mended, and there had been other boyfriends, other youthful squabbles from which they had also recovered. They'd been kids, barely nineteen, and Madison had thought the incident was long behind them, but apparently BiBi had never entirely forgotten. Or forgiven?

"Let's just leave that in the past, shall we?" she asked somewhat stiffly. "I promise I won't do anything to ruin your wedding weekend, BiBi. Now, do you want a cookie or not?"

Grimacing in what might have been a slightly apologetic manner, BiBi spoke quickly. "Yes, sure. Thanks."

Madison made a point not to even glance in Jason's direction when she walked to the food table for the desserts. What was it about a wedding, she wondered in exasperation, that could turn the most intelligent, levelheaded people into players in a soap opera?

* * *

Back at the arena area, several activities were planned for the remainder of the afternoon. Groups assembled on the grounds for horse-shoes, archery and roping lessons. For later amusement, a mechanical bull sat within a rope ring, surrounded by padded flooring to cushion the inevitable tumbles. Inside the arena, barrels and poles were being lined up for timed events prior to the dinner campfire. Once again, Madison was impressed with the ranch's efficiency in entertaining the diverse group of guests. There really did seem to be something for everyone, even those who'd initially balked at the idea of a day on a dude ranch.

Madison joined several women lining up for archery lessons, which sounded like fun. BiBi and Corinna were among the group. Madison wasn't sure what Jason was doing; she was making such an effort not to look at him that she'd lost track of him. She suspected he was participating in one of the noisy horseshoes tournaments.

Allen hurried to stand behind Madison when she lifted the bow to her shoulder after a rudimentary demonstration. "Want me to help you aim that, Maddie?"

He seemed eager to stand behind her with his arms around her to support the bow. She wasn't sure whether it was because he was especially attracted to her or just liked the idea of being the gallant male, but either way, she didn't want his assistance. She was quite capable of pulling the string back herself. Nor had she ever invited him to call her Maddie, she added silently. Berating herself for being grumpy—which she couldn't help but blame, just a little, on BiBi—she made an effort to respond politely. "Thank you, but I'd like to try it on my own."

Despite her attempt to be gracious, it was obvious that he wasn't pleased she'd declined his most recent offer of assistance. "Yeah, sure. No problem. I'll just go help Hannah."

"Yes, you should do that." Maybe Hannah would be more appreciative.

"Bet you'd have let D'Alessandro help," she heard Allen grumble as he moved away.

Madison grimaced, hoping neither BiBi nor Corinna had overheard his disgruntled remark, though she suspected that Corinna had caught the gist of it. She blew a short breath out her nose as she took her stance to raise her bow toward the hay-bale target several yards ahead of her. More junior high drama. Great.

If she ever married, she promised herself, letting the arrow fly, she was going to elope.

The mechanical bull was unleashed after the games. A trained operator sat at the controls, overseeing the speed and spin direction of the automated ride. The operator took it easy on the true novices, though he was quick to toss them once they started to assert a bit of confidence in maintaining their seat on the twisting, bucking "bull." Wearing helmets for safety, the riders landed on the padded flooring surrounding the device, wincing in chagrin, then standing to take a bow for the laughing, applauding onlookers sitting on folding bleachers set around the bull ring.

Madison was talked into trying it. Self-consciously avoiding looking at anyone in particular among the audience, she settled onto the back of the bull-shaped machine, sliding her right hand beneath the neck rope as she was instructed by Mickey, who helped her mount. Her left arm was to be used for balance, he informed her.

"Ready?"

She drew a deep breath, letting the cheers and encouragement from the other guests wash over her. "Ready as I'm going to be."

The operator was gentle with her at first. It wasn't easy to hold on, but she thought she was getting the hang of it—until a clever twist and buck sent her flying through the air before she'd even realized she'd left the machine. She landed in an ignominious heap, breathless but uninjured. She couldn't stop laughing as she rose to take the obligatory bow. The spectators clapped and hooted in good-natured teasing.

A few of the men and a couple of the women had obviously ridden bulls, either real or mechanical, before. They were given the full treatment by the grinning operator, trying to hang on for the eight-second count that would be required of a rodeo bull rider. Somewhat to Madison's surprise, Corinna was among that group.

"She's ridden bulls?" she asked BiBi disbelievingly when Corinna walked into the ring as one of the experienced riders.

"Mechanical only," BiBi replied. "She went through a phase in college where she and some of her friends hit the bars every weekend to ride the bulls and shoot pool. She actually made some money betting beer-soaked frat boys she could hang on to the bulls longer than they could. Dad would have locked her in her room if he'd ever found out about it," she added with a laugh. "As it was, he had to threaten to stop paying her tuition if she didn't buckle down and study more and party less."

Madison remembered BiBi talking about her younger sister's penchant for parties, but this was the first she'd heard of the bull riding. She wondered if perhaps Corinna had also kept that pastime secret from her older sister back then. It was amazing Corinna had managed to graduate with grades high enough to get her into pharmacy school if she'd really been as lax with her studies as BiBi implied. BiBi had always said her younger sister was brilliant, if a little flaky.

Madison wondered if her own older siblings said the same about her. Maybe she and Corinna had a bit more in common than she'd realized. Madison had never ridden mechanical bulls for cash, but she'd pulled a few crazy youthful stunts in college, making her mother and siblings shake their heads in exasperation on more than one occasion.

Corinna proved quickly that she hadn't forgotten the skills she had learned making bets with the fraternity boys. She settled onto the bull with visible assurance, tossing her dark hair and posing in a way that demonstrated she enjoyed the attention. Madison noticed Brandon McCafferty crowding close to the rope barrier. He seemed unable to look away from Corinna as the device began a slow, bobbing rotation and she swayed sensually atop it, her left arm seeming to float in the air beside her, her breasts straining against her blouse as she arched her back to maintain her position.

Brandon's Adam's apple bobbed in his lean throat with a hard swallow Madison could see from several feet away. A few of the other men moved instinctively closer for a better vantage point, to the indulgent exasperation of a few wives and girlfriends.

Madison couldn't resist turning her head just slightly to locate Jason. She wondered if he was as mesmerized as the other single—and not-so-single—male onlookers. She spotted him sitting on a bench to her right.

He wasn't looking at Corinna. He was looking straight back at her.

Chapter Five

When their eyes met, Jason touched his hat, his lips quirking into a slight smile. Madison wondered if every time she looked at him during the remainder of the weekend, her gaze would be drawn to his very nice mouth. If every time she saw his lips, she would immediately be inundated with memories of how they had felt pressed to hers.

That's what she got for being reckless, she chided herself as she looked quickly away. Weren't her siblings always warning her that her impulsiveness would get her in trouble someday? She doubted that Meagan would have kissed a stranger in a moonlit garden, leading to all sorts of awkwardness the following day.

Madison had always been the slightly different one in her family. Both her siblings had become surgeons; she'd chosen psychiatry, a much different type of practice. She always teasingly said it was because psychiatry required less time and effort than surgery, which everyone knew was a grueling career. The truth was, of course, that psychiatry had its own demands and challenges that simply appealed to her nature more than surgery. She'd actually considered forgoing medical school altogether and going to graduate school for psychology, a completely different path than her sister and brother, but had decided rather at the last hour to accept the offer from the state medical school. She still wasn't quite sure whether she'd done so because she truly wanted the medical training or because she had allowed herself to be so influenced by Meagan and Mitch and their mother, who had all urged her to pursue the medical degree.

Now she was the only one in the family still single, still spending many of her weekends at parties with friends, still living in a rented apartment with odds and ends of furniture, still uncertain of her career future when they'd each had their own career paths mapped out almost from the day they'd entered primary school.

She wondered if Jason would agree with her siblings. Mr. Responsibility, BiBi had called him. Settled and sedate, she had implied. None of which sounded like what Madison was looking for—if she had been looking, of course. She was probably no more his ideal match, if he were in the market for a mate. A weekend fling would have been all they'd have had together, had other circumstances not made that so problematic.

She'd have happily settled for that fling, she thought with a faintly wistful sigh. Her brother's and sister's certain disapproval notwithstanding, it wasn't every day a girl had the chance to have her teeth rattled by a charming, handsome stranger. Madison hated to have to pass up such a tempting opportunity.

A burst of cheers brought her attention back to the bull ring where Corinna had just landed gracefully on the mat after finally being tossed from the device by the grinning operator. She'd lasted six and a half seconds into the rodeo-level ride, longer than anyone yet. Madison saw her glance in Jason's direction as she took her sweeping bow.

Madison's teeth would remain unrattled this weekend. Nor would she spend the next two days pining over Jason like Corinna. And she wouldn't use Allen to avoid him, the way she suspected Corinna was using hapless Brandon. Madison was perfectly capable of having a great time without a man by her side, as she'd been doing for most of her twenty-eight years. She could certainly do so for two more days.

Pole bending and barrel racing followed the mechanical bull riding. For those not inclined to ride in the events or watch from the arena bleachers, Gayla was giving rudimentary roping lessons. More archery lessons were also available or the guests could make a beaded bookmark or keychain in a Western crafts session. Something for everyone, indeed, Jason thought drily, joining the small group getting ready to start the pole bending timed runs.

He would ride Pablo in the event, which consisted of completing a cloverleaf pattern around three poles without knocking them down. The competitor who finished in the fastest time would be named the winner. He hadn't competed in many riding events, but his cousins had sometimes organized this type of race at his uncle's ranch just for fun. He supposed he could hold his own among this group.

An hour later, he held a second-place trophy, a gaudy, oversized, gold-toned plastic figure of a mounted cowboy on a rather oddly shaped horse on a faux-marble stand. He studied it with a lifted eyebrow, rather relieved he hadn't won first place, since that trophy was slightly larger. Mike Campbell, one of the other groomsmen, had taken that prize by less than half a second faster than Jason's time. Catching Jason's eye over the top of the big trophy, Mike smiled ruefully.

Jason spoke in a wry drawl to the victor. "Congratulations on your win."

Mike chuckled. "Yeah. Uh, same to you. Going to display that in your medical offices?"

"I will if you'll put that one in your law office," Jason retorted without hesitation.

Laughing, Mike shook his head. "I think I'll let my older son have this one. He's five. It'll thrill him to have a real cowboy trophy—the closest he's going to get from me."

"It doesn't seem fair to deprive your younger boy of a trophy," Jason replied immediately. "I think you should let him have this one, just so he won't feel left out."

Mike chuckled again. "I know what you're doing. But I'll take it off your hands, anyway. You're right, Nicholas would probably love to have a trophy like his big brother."

Jason promptly handed over the heavy plastic prize. Balancing one in each arm, Mike carried them off to share with his wife to take to their boys later.

"That was very generous of you."

Hearing Madison's voice, he turned his head quickly. He was somewhat disappointed to find her standing next to BiBi, giving him that same rather distant smile she used whenever anyone else was nearby.

"He thought his boys would get a kick out of

the trophies," he said, choosing his words carefully so as not to offend BiBi by implying that he didn't appreciate the award. "They can use them to decorate their rooms."

BiBi didn't seem miffed by his gesture. "I'm sure they will love them. Congratulations on second place. I watched your ride. You were very good."

"Thanks. I nearly knocked over one of the poles. Uncle Jared would have given me a hard time about not sitting the saddle more firmly so I could guide Pablo with my legs."

BiBi smiled. "I met your uncle Jared a couple of times. I bet he was a tough teacher."

"A great one, though." Like most of the members of his mother's family, Jason pretty much idolized the oldest Walker brother, a tough-talking, tenderhearted rancher who'd spent the past twenty-odd years taking in at-risk boys and raising them with his generous, nurturing wife, Cassie. He was a hard taskmaster, but most of the boys left the ranch wanting to be just like him.

"Did you see Corinna take first place in the barrel races?" BiBi asked a bit too offhandedly. "She had a great ride. She was sure Toni Blanchard would win because Toni used to compete in junior rodeo, but I guess Toni had an off day, or Corinna had a really good one."

"I saw her," Jason agreed lightly. "I guess she didn't forget everything she learned in all those riding lessons during summer vacations."

BiBi nodded, as though expressing her approval that he'd remembered those lessons. "Jason's family and ours have known each other all our lives," she said for Madison's benefit. "We all have so many shared memories, don't we, Jason?"

Jason shot a quick glance at Madison, seeing a flicker of exasperation cross her face before she schooled her expression.

He'd been an idiot, he realized abruptly. He'd

been unable to understand why Madison's behavior toward him had changed so suddenly. Now, seeing her with BiBi, it was starting to make sense.

"Yes," he said, trying to keep his tone equable. "I think of you and Corinna almost like more cousins among the big D'Alessandro clan."

"Oh. Well." BiBi stumbled a little, almost humorous in her realization that her comments hadn't accomplished quite what she'd had in mind. "We aren't—"

Jason's phone buzzed from the holder on his belt. He reached for it and checked the ID screen. "That's my office. I should probably take it. Excuse me, ladies."

He turned away, telling himself he and Madison could talk later. In private, he hoped.

Dinner was served on round tables covered with red-and-white gingham tablecloths and set in a circle around a blazing bonfire. While the guests indulged in barbecue and "fixin's" or vegetarian entrees and salads, they were serenaded by a more than decent cowboy band. Several of the hands who'd helped out during the day turned out to be musicians, as well. Madison was delighted to see Mickey sawing a bow across a battered fiddle. She knew he wouldn't call it a violin.

She sat at a table with the Polanskis and Hannah Thatcher, leaving two empty chairs on the other side of the table from Madison. Allen Burleson slid into the seat next to Hannah, flirting with her in a way that soon had her blushing and giggling. Seated between Lila and Hannah, Madison was glad Allen's attentions had moved away from herself. Hannah seemed to enjoy the attention, and if it bothered her that he'd flirted with Madison first, she didn't let it show.

Madison was chatting with Lila about the day's events when she heard Jason's voice. "Is this seat taken?" he asked, addressing the group as a whole when he nodded toward the empty chair between Allen and Tommy.

Everyone at the table, with the exception of Madison, spoke in unison to invite him to join them. Realizing her silence could be taken as rudeness, she quickly added her own welcome. He gave her a quick look and an almost imperceptible nod, then slid into the chair.

When he spoke, it was to ask Lila, "How are you? Have you had a good time today?"

"I've had a lovely time," she replied eagerly. "Did you see my Tommy ride the bull? Seven and a half seconds!"

"I saw. Great job, Tom. I only made it to six," Jason answered with a wry chuckle. "The operator gave me a ride that darned near dislocated my shoulder."

"I made it to seven," Allen said with no little pride. "He pushed it hard for me, too, but I held on. Thought I'd go the whole eight, but my hand slipped on the rope. I think it might have gotten a little loose with the riders before me."

"Great job, Allen," Jason conceded easily. "Mike held on for the eight-count. I guess he was the only one who did so today."

Lila shifted in her chair, something she'd been doing since Madison had sat beside her.

"Are you uncomfortable?" Madison asked her quietly.

Lila grimaced somewhat apologetically. "I'm always uncomfortable these days," she admitted. "I might have overdone it a little today. My back is really hurting."

"Can I get you anything, honey?" Tommy asked, his expression solicitous. "They've got hot water and tea bags on the drinks table. A hot drink usually helps you relax."

Lila beamed at him. "That would be perfect, thanks, sweetie."

He touched her hair when he stood to fetch the drink. A brief, light, almost absentminded stroke that still spoke volumes about his feelings for his pregnant wife, as far as Madison was concerned. She'd seen her brother touch his adored bride in much the same manner, and Seth do the same with Meagan. Just a fleeting moment of private connection in an otherwise public venue. Sweet, she thought with a silent sigh. Maybe someday someone would connect with her that way.

She focused intently on her dinner after that random thought, telling herself not to be like everyone else and get too carried away with all this wedding stuff.

"So what's the plan after dinner?" Allen asked while they were eating desserts—a choice of several fruit cobblers with freshly made soft-serve ice cream. "Are we headed back to the hotel soon?"

Pressing a hand to her side, Lila pushed her dessert away barely tasted. "No, there's an hour of group singing and storytelling around the campfire before we head back."

"Oh." Allen looked more resigned than enthusiastic. "BiBi sure planned a full day, didn't she?"

"You up to another hour, honey?" Tommy asked, studying his wife's face with increasing concern. "You're looking pretty pale."

Madison had just been thinking the same thing. Something about Lila's expression didn't look quite right to her. She suspected the woman was in more discomfort than she was letting on. "Are you okay, Lila?"

Hand still pressed to her lower side, Lila nodded, but without a great deal of assurance. "The pain in my back is getting worse," she confessed. "Maybe if someone could find me a more padded chair or something? I'm sure I'll be fine—I don't want to ruin the evening for everyone else."

"Don't you worry about that," Madison told her. "Maybe we should take you inside the ranch house. I was told there are rooms in there for dining and dancing and other activities when the weather's too bad for outdoor events. I bet there's a couch or at least an easy chair you can use to rest before the bus ride back to the hotel."

Privately she wondered if Tommy shouldn't arrange different transportation for his wife. The bus didn't seem to be the most comfortable conveyance, as nice as it had been.

Buck, the ranch host, appeared at their side, and Madison realized that Jason had signaled him. "Something I can do for you?" Buck asked.

Giving Jason a glance of gratitude, Madison repeated her suggestion for a comfortable place for Lila to rest. Lila demurred again, visibly self-conscious with the attention, but Buck nodded obligingly. "Of course. If you'll follow me, ma'am and sir, I'll find you a comfy place to hang out for the next hour and a half or so until we load the buses. We've got a nice lounge area inside, and I'll have someone bring you some herbal tea, if you'd like."

Tommy and Lila stood to follow him. On an instinct, Madison rose with them. "Maybe I can help you inside?"

Both of the Polanskis smiled gratefully. "You can take her other side," Tommy said, clinging to his wife's left arm.

Madison nodded and looped her left arm with Lila's right. Once they were inside, she would suggest that Tommy call a cab to take them back to Dallas. It wouldn't be cheap, but she'd tactfully offer to pitch in, if necessary, and she was sure others would, too. Lila needed to get off her feet as soon as possible and take it easy for the remainder of the weekend.

They didn't even make it to the ranch house before Lila cried out and doubled over in pain. Tommy reacted in panic, clutching at his wife's arm with a white-knuckled grip. "Honey? What's wrong? What's happening?"

Though Lila's maternity jeans were a dark denim, Madison could still see the darker stain that was rapidly spreading down her legs. Her heart sank. It had been five years since her rotation in obstetrics and gynecology. She only hoped she remembered everything she had learned then.

She looked at Buck, trying to keep her voice calm for the sake of the anxious couple. "You should call for an ambulance now."

Lila cried out again, sagging heavily between her husband and Madison. "I think my water broke. But it's too soon. The baby's not due for another month."

People began chattering excitedly behind them, but Madison focused solely on Lila and Tommy, who had gone stark white with fear. "It's okay," she began.

"I'm a doctor. I can help."

Jason and Madison had spoken almost in unison, coincidentally choosing the same words to reassure the couple. Skidding to a stop after rushing toward them, Jason looked at Madison in bemusement when her words registered. She'd known he was a doctor, but apparently, no one had mentioned her career to him.

"You're a doctor?"

She nodded. "Psychiatry. Please tell me you're ob-gyn."

His lips twitched. "Internal medicine. No obstetrics, but I'm sure between the two of us we can remember the basics, if necessary."

"Let's just hope the ambulance gets here before that becomes necessary," she murmured, turning back to her—their—patient.

Tommy, Jason and Allen carried Lila inside the roomy ranch house where bright lights and an open floor plan welcomed them into the main lounge area decorated in cowboy chic. Called in to assist, Gayla swiftly produced a stack of clean sheets and towels from the supplies for the cabins used for dude ranch guests staying longer than a day.

Once Lila was settled on top of several folded sheets covering a wide vinyl sofa, Allen swiftly excused himself.

"Don't either of you try to leave," Tommy ordered Madison and Jason. "I want both of you here in case the ambulance doesn't arrive in time."

"It usually takes several hours for a first baby to be born," Madison assured him, mentally crossing her fingers. "I'm guessing there will be plenty of time."

Lila wailed and clutched her middle, drawing her knees upward in pain.

Okay, maybe not, Madison thought, swallowing hard as she looked at Jason. "Should we, um…?"

He nodded somberly. "Buck said the nearest hospital is almost half an hour away. We should probably do a quick exam."

Asking Buck to keep everyone else outside, they covered Lila with a sheet from the waist down. Tommy helped her undress beneath the sheet while Madison and Jason scrubbed their hands in a small lavatory that opened off the lounge.

"I didn't realize you're a doctor," Jason said as he lathered forcefully from the container of liquid soap provided for guests.

"Fourth-year resident. I'll be starting a child and adolescent psych fellowship next year. I just found out this morning that you're in practice when, um, someone mentioned your connection to the Lovato family."

"About that connection—"

It was almost a relief when they were interrupted by another wail from Lila and a shout for help from Tommy. "Y'all need to hurry! She's hurting bad."

This was not the time to talk about themselves, Madison thought with a quick shake of her head. Holding her scrubbed-clean hands in front of her chest out of long-forged habit, she hurried back into the other room with Jason close behind her.

Jason made it clear he thought Madison should do the exam. "I'll stand by if you need me."

She gave him a "gee, thanks" look, but since Lila was tearily begging for help, she had no other choice.

It was obvious that the Polanski baby was in a hurry to be born. Madison looked at Jason over the sheet covering Lila's raised knees. "We don't have time to wait for the ambulance."

Lila moaned and Tommy went a shade paler, which Madison wouldn't have thought possible. She frowned at Jason and nodded toward Tommy. Catching her meaning—or maybe he'd already noticed for himself—Jason spoke bracingly to the other man, reminding him that two doctors were there to help and the ambulance was on its way.

"But it's too soon," Lila kept repeating, her voice catching in frightened little sobs.

"Don't you worry about that," Madison said reassuringly. "Lots of babies are born at eight months and do very well. I happened to have been a couple weeks early, myself. My family said it's because I've always been too impatient to wait my turn for anything. Maybe little Polanski here is the same way."

Her light tone seemed to accomplish what she'd hoped. Lila looked somewhat reassured when she gasped out, "Joseph. His name is Joseph. After Tommy's daddy."

"That's a very nice name. Jason and I will take good care of you and Joseph until the ambulance gets here, okay?"

Lila's eyes went wide as her entire body shuddered. "I need to push."

"Oh, honey, can't you wait a little longer?"

"No, I can't wait!" she snapped at her worried husband. "Get over here and start doing that coaching thing. And you," she added to Jason, "stop fussing over T[...] will you?"

Jason obviously knew b[...] though he and Madison shared [...] look at this sudden change in t[...] sunny, mild-mannered woman they'd [...]

The EMTs arrived some fifteen minute[...] young Joseph emerged. Because it was too [...] to load Lila into the ambulance, they waited nearby with the ambulance incubator while Madison and Jason completed the delivery. Madison was grateful to have them—and their supplies—at hand during the final stages. She and Jason worked effortlessly together, barely having to speak to each other as they coordinated their movements, both encouraging Lila and Tommy during the process. By unspoken agreement, Madison took over as primary delivery doctor while Jason performed the nurse duties. When Joseph was out and the cord cut, ile she fin-

r her own
of her eye
both con-
few tense
t they all
e to clear
ndignant

mmy and help Madison,

tter than to laugh,
a quick, amused
ne from the
net earlier.
before
late

"He's a little scrawny, but he looks good," Jason assured the anxious parents while the medics rushed forward to begin transport procedures. "As far as I can tell from my preliminary examination, he's going to be just fine."

Tommy and Lila stared at their son with tear-streaked faces expressing exhaustion, stress, awe and instant, unconditional love. Madison blinked back a few stray tears of her own. She had almost forgotten how much she'd enjoyed that part of her labor and delivery rotation, though she still preferred the specialty she had chosen.

The medics took the fussing baby from his parents to secure him inside the ambulance incubator where he'd be safe and warm for the trip to the hospital. And then Lila was transferred to a gurney and wheeled out to the ambulance with Tommy walking alongside her, holding her hand. Gayla and a couple of other ranch employees had already begun cleanup in the lounge, and Madison suspected that within a very short time, there would be no evidence of the events that had taken place here.

Exhausted herself now, she turned to Jason when the Polanski family was out of their sight.

"Oh. My. Gosh," she said with an exaggerated wipe of her forehead. "That was not the way I expected to wrap up the day's events."

Looking a little peaked, as well, he gave her a lopsided grin. "You and me both. I'm just glad you were here."

"Right. So you could hand off the messy part to me."

He nodded. "I won't argue with you. L and D was never my forte."

"Mine, either. Head doc, remember?" She tapped her forehead. "Whole different end of the patient."

Jason laughed and reached out seemingly on impulse to give her a bracing squeeze around the shoulders. "You did good, Doc Esmeralda."

"You did good, yourself, Dr. Jones," she conceded, letting her head rest against his shoulder just for one weak moment. The experience they had just shared only added to the unexpected— and decidedly inconvenient—bond that had formed between them at last night's party.

Still determined to keep peace with BiBi, she promised herself she would hold him at arm's length again. In just a moment.

"Oh, wow, we just saw Lila and Tommy and the baby onto the ambulance. They're on the way to the hospital now. You two really—" Seeing Madison standing in the circle of Jason's arm, BiBi stopped abruptly in the doorway of the lounge, her excited words trailing off.

Madison stepped quickly away from Jason just as Carl and Corinna appeared behind BiBi. She was pretty sure Corinna hadn't seen anything—not that there had been anything to see, she reminded herself impatiently.

"Jason and I were just congratulating each other on remembering our med school training. Although he made me do most of the work," she added with a teasing scowl.

Jason grinned and reached for the cowboy hat he'd tossed onto a chair earlier. "Delivering babies is women's work," he drawled, settling the hat onto his head. "Us cowboys just pass out cigars afterward. Anyone got any cigars?"

Madison snorted and swept toward the door. "We'd better get out of here now, before we step in any of that manure he's shoveling," she told

BiBi, linking arms with her friend and winking at Corinna. "Come on, I'll tell you all about my brilliant doctoring during the bus ride back to the hotel."

Either she'd reassured them with her joking toward Jason, or maybe the fact that she didn't even glance back at him as they walked away, or the sisters were simply too interested in hearing all the particulars about little Joseph's birth to focus on how friendly Madison and Jason had become during the delivery. They stopped giving her searching glances and started peppering her with questions that didn't stop all the way back to the hotel. Others on the bus wanted to know all the details, as well, so Madison ended up telling the story several times. She was careful each time to focus more on her own involvement with Lila, keeping Tommy and Jason in the background of the tale and of roughly equal importance.

"So you just handed the baby to Jason?"

someone asked after the second—or was it the third?—recounting. "All messy and squirmy and everything?"

"He had a towel to wrap the baby in."

Several of the women listening from surrounding bus seats looked intrigued. Madison suspected they were picturing handsome Jason D'Alessandro holding a newborn infant. She had to admit she had found his competent, gentle handling of the tiny baby attractive—but that was hardly a surprise, since she'd been charmed by pretty much everything else she'd observed about Jason so far that weekend.

"Well, he is a family practice physician," Hannah pointed out logically. "I'm sure he's used to holding infants."

"He's always liked kids," Corinna added. "He has three younger siblings, two young nephews, and too many cousins to count, and all the little ones love Jason."

"So, did Tommy pass out?" BiBi asked quickly,

either to distract her sister from thoughts of Jason with children or to distract everyone else from noticing Corinna's besotted tone. Maybe both. "He looked pretty pale when you all rushed him and Lila into the ranch house."

"No, he held up great. He was a little nervous at first, but J— But he calmed down fairly quickly." She had almost praised Jason's skillful soothing of Tommy's anxiety but had changed her words at the last moment. Saint Jason had received enough credit this evening, she decided. Seriously, the guy had to have some flaws. Corinna's crush aside, and discounting the few minor imperfections BiBi had listed, no one could be as perfect as Jason D'Alessandro was beginning to sound.

Madison had never been particularly interested in too-perfect people—another reason she had chosen psychiatry as a specialty. Maybe that was the solution to her problematic fascination with Jason. The more she learned about how upstand-

ing and responsible he was, the more she realized how different he was from the rebel she'd
fantasized him to be after last night's masquerade, the less intrigued she would be by him.

A few people wandered toward the bar when
the buses deposited them back at the hotel.
Madison headed straight for the elevators. It
had been a long, exhausting day and she was
ready for some downtime. BiBi had another busy
day scheduled for tomorrow, followed by the
wedding and the flight back home on Sunday,
followed by work early Monday morning, so
Madison figured she'd better rest while she had
the chance.

Stripping out of her clothes, she took a quick
shower, letting the hot water soothe her weary
muscles. She would probably be reminded of
that long trail ride tomorrow, she thought with
a slight grimace.

Slipping into her favorite thigh-length, black
sheath nightgown decorated with touches of

lace and red embroidery, she dried her honey-blond hair and left it loose around her shoulders, automatically examining the roots to see if it were time for a touch-up. Both she and her sister were in the habit of lightening the mousy-brown hair they had inherited from their father.

Turning her head from side to side and studying the reflection in the mirror, Madison wondered if she should go a little lighter next time. Or maybe she should add some red to the mix. Something completely different. She had rather enjoyed being in costume last night, changing up her appearance from the fashionable, yet maybe too predictable style she'd fallen into during the past couple of years.

As her fourth year of her demanding residency drew closer to an end, maybe it was time to shake up her routines a little. Let herself get a little reckless again, closer to the footloose, impulsive fun-lover she'd once been. Oh, she wasn't going to go wild or anything, she assured herself, reaching for her rose-scented body lotion. She was still a physician, and she would perform her duties with the same conscientious dedication as always—but she had to remember that it was important for her to have a life away from work, too. Maybe if she spent a little more time having fun, she'd be less susceptible to a pair of gleaming dark eyes and a roguish smile, more able to put that sexy grin out of her mind when it became clear that it was time to move on.

A soft tap on her door derailed her musings and made her turn quickly on the vanity chair. She certainly wasn't expecting company at this hour.

BiBi, she thought with shake of her head, reaching for the short robe that matched her gown. Who else could it be?

If her friend was here to chew her out again for getting too friendly with Jason, Madison was going to have a harder time keeping her temper. Leaving the belt of her robe untied, she stalked barefoot toward the door. What was she supposed to have done, refused to help deliver Lila's baby because Jason's assistance was also required? It just so happened that both Madison and Jason were doctors. If BiBi refused to accept that as the simple coincidence it was, then she…

Madison's breath caught in her throat when she glanced automatically through the security peephole in the door. Her caller wasn't BiBi.

After only a momentary hesitation, she turned the locks and opened the door a crack.

"Have you wandered onto the wrong floor, Dr. Jones?" she asked, the sudden huskiness of her voice making the lame quip even less effective.

Jason's smile did not reach his intense, dark eyes. "I hope not."

Pausing only a few heartbeats longer, Madison made her decision. She stepped back in silent invitation.

Jason slipped inside the room, closing the door behind him with a quiet, firm click.

Chapter Six

"Before you say anything," Jason said as soon as he was in the room, "there's something you should know about my connection to BiBi and Corinna."

"Your families have a longtime connection and wouldn't mind seeing that bond formalized with a match between their offspring. They've decided you and Corinna make a nice couple. Corinna tends to agree, but you don't think of her in that way."

"Oh." Jason blinked a couple of times as if

trying to think of something to say now that she had summarized the speech she assumed he'd been prepared to make. "Well, yeah. Something like that."

She shrugged. "I picked up clues from things said during the past couple of days."

"Either a lot was said or you're very perceptive. You summed it up almost perfectly."

"I do like to think I'm perceptive. That's part of my job, after all."

"Psychiatry."

She nodded.

"I'd like to hear all about that—eventually." He took a step toward her, searching her face questioningly.

She was keenly aware that she stood in front of him in a short nightie, a thin, open robe and bare legs and feet. He, too, had showered and changed since returning from the ranch. His dark hair was still just a little damp and he had swapped his Western wear for a pale blue shirt with loose khakis and brown slip-ons. Much more average and conservative clothing than what she'd seen him wear before—so why did she still find him so exciting?

"So you understand that I'm completely free to spend time with anyone I like?" he persisted. "You weren't pushing me away today because you thought I was involved with someone else?"

"I didn't exactly push you away."

The look he gave her told her he knew better. "You made it clear enough that you wanted me to keep a distance. I didn't know if that was because you didn't want to cause gossip or because someone had warned you off or because you'd just lost interest, but I figured the only way to find out for sure was just to flat out ask you. I don't mean to make you uncomfortable showing up at your door this way, so if you want me to go, just say the word."

"I would love for you to stay awhile," she answered with characteristic candor.

His expression lightening, he took another step forward.

She raised a hand, palm toward him. "However—"

He stopped, his smile fading again.

"I'm here this weekend for BiBi. She's been my friend for a long time and I'm very fond of her. She's planned every detail of this wedding so carefully and so eagerly. I would never do anything to put a cloud over it for her."

He frowned. "Neither would I. But I don't see how—"

"Upsetting Corinna would upset BiBi, too. And, well, BiBi and I have a little baggage from the past that I don't want to pop up again. You seem to have made it clear—in a nice way, from what I gathered—that you don't want to get tangled up with Corinna. Putting moves on me this weekend, instead, could be taken as a slap to her face."

His expression was a cross between frustration and grim amusement. "Putting the moves on you? Is that what I've been doing?"

Her own mouth twitched. "Yes, Dr. Jones, I would say you did."

She didn't have to clarify by mentioning the kiss in the garden. The way his gaze lingered on her faint smile told her he, too, was remembering that particular move. "And if you hadn't decided I'd be too much trouble, would those moves have been effective? Just for my own curiosity."

She sighed a little. "They were most definitely effective."

He inched a little closer. "Madison—"

This time when she raised her hand, it landed on his chest. She left it there, savoring the warmth that seeped through his shirt and into her palm. "You are certainly trouble."

He covered her fingers with his own, and the warmth spread into her arm and beyond. "Is it wrong that I rather like you seeing me in that way?"

"Oh, I think you could be underestimating yourself." Her voice had a slightly husky edge to it now.

Lifting his free hand, he stroked a fingertip along the line of her jaw. "Maybe I'm just different with you."

If he didn't kiss her soon, she was going to melt into a puddle right at his feet, she thought with a swallow. She might just do that even if he did kiss her. She was pretty sure she was about to find out.

Leaning toward him, she spoke with her mouth almost touching his. "Whatever it is, I'm finding it very difficult to resist your particular type of trouble. Just do me one favor, will you?"

His arms were already around her waist, gently tugging her closer so that their bodies met. There was no doubt that he was feeling as reckless and hungry as she was, but he held back just long enough to mutter, "Name it."

"Let's just keep whatever happens private. Our own secret weekend adventure. Even though we don't have to sneak around behind anyone's back, exactly, I'd prefer to keep this just between the two of us."

Jason brushed his lips against hers, making her crave more. "I have no problem with that."

Somewhat reassured that she could have her cake—wedding cake, as it were—without hurting anyone else, she wrapped her arms around his neck. "Then kiss me, Jones."

He groaned. "With pleasure, Esmeralda."

Teasing quickly sizzled into passion when he crushed his mouth against hers. She crowded as close to him as she could get, parting her lips to grant him as many liberties as he chose to take. He accepted the invitation eagerly, dipping his tongue into her welcoming mouth to explore with a scientist's thoroughness and claim with an adventurer's boldness.

With her robe parted, only his clothing and her thin satin nightgown lay between them. Even that barrier was too much. She wanted to savor the athletic body she had so admired when he'd worn nothing but swim trunks. Sliding a hand between them, she fumbled with buttons even as Jason pushed at her robe, slipping it off her shoulders and letting it drop to the floor around her bare feet.

The image of his beautiful chest had flitted through the back of her mind all day, taunting her even as she had admired him in his sexy Western wear. When she had seen him in the pool—had it been only that morning?—she had wanted to run her hands all over him, to explore and admire every nicely defined muscle, to press her mouth to his skin and see if he tasted as yummy as he looked. Now that they had complete privacy, she allowed herself those liberties, sliding her palms slowly from his shoulders to his narrow waist, flicking the tip of her tongue against one flat brown nipple until she teased a low groan from his throat.

His hands tightened spasmodically at her hips, then slipped lower to grab the hem of her nightgown and tug upward. She raised her arms. In one smooth move, he swept the gown over her head and tossed it aside, leaving her clad only in a pair of black lace panties. It had been a while since she'd been this intimate with anyone, but she didn't feel particularly self-conscious with Jason. The unmistakable appreciation in his expression as he looked at her was quite the ego booster.

She'd have much more freedom to explore—and be explored—on the bed. Taking his hand with a smile, she turned to lead him there. She planted a hand on his chest and gave a playful shove, and he cooperated by tumbling onto the bed that had already been made ready for her to climb into. He reached for her, but she evaded his hands long enough to unzip a compartment in her carry-on bag and pull out a few sealed packets. She hadn't expected to need protection this weekend, but she was glad now that she was in the habit of always carrying some in her luggage. Tossing the packets onto the bed with Jason, she dove into his waiting arms.

His hands and mouth were already moving eagerly over her almost before she stretched out beside him. Her black lace panties joined his clothing in a jumbled pile by the bed. After kissing a slow, thorough, mind-emptying path from her mouth to her throat to her breasts, he nibbled his way from her rib cage to the top of her thigh, both tickling and further arousing her. Locking her hands in his dark hair, she squirmed and giggled breathlessly. His husky chuckle made her breath catch hard in her throat. His left hand moved to the inside of her thigh and the breath shot out in a gasp.

Jason lifted his head suddenly, and he stared at her right hip. "You have a tattoo."

She couldn't help giggling again. He'd sounded for all the world as if he were telling her something she didn't already know. "Yes, I was there when it was inked."

He traced a fingertip gently over the thumb-size fairy that hovered just above her right hip joint. "You continue to surprise me."

Shifting her weight, she pushed him onto his back and climbed on top of him. "I'm just getting started, Dr. Jones."

A groan rumbled deep in his chest as he reached for her. "By all means, continue."

Lowering herself slowly onto him, she leaned over to speak against his parted lips. "With pleasure."

Though he was tired, Jason wasn't ready for sleep. Morning would arrive all too soon, and with it, a long day of scheduled activities during which he would have to keep his distance from Madison. She'd made it clear enough that he was to do nothing to suggest he'd spent any more time with her than any of the other members of the wedding party. He would keep his word— but he already knew it would be very hard to be in the same room with her without wanting to touch her. Or even just gaze at her, as he was doing now, propped on one arm and lying on his side next to her.

She lay against her pillow, her honey hair tossed appealingly around her face, her cheeks flushed from their lovemaking. She wore no makeup, but her lips were rosy and a little pouty from his kisses. The skin of her throat and the upper curve of her breasts above the snowy sheets glistened faintly from exertion.

They had been rather energetic, he thought with a surge of thoroughly masculine satisfaction. Now he would be content to just lie there looking at her for hours yet.

She opened her eyes, giving him a sweet, lazy smile that made him change his mind. He was quite sure he'd want to do more than just look once he'd had a chance to recover a bit.

"You're staring at me, Dr. Jones."

He really did love it when she called him that. Silly, maybe, but she was just so darned appealing when she teased him with their own private joke. "It's hard to look away from perfection."

She laughed softly, shaking her head against the pillow. "And you tried to pretend you don't have 'moves.' If that wasn't a practiced line, I don't know what it would be."

It would be the truth, he thought, but he merely smiled.

She nestled more comfortably into her pillow. "Hmm. I think I'm going to feel that ride tomorrow."

Jason chuckled.

She punched him lightly in the chest. "I meant the trail ride."

"Yes. I knew that," he said, tongue in cheek.

"You are so bad."

Never in his life had Jason D'Alessandro been seen as a bad boy. Even though she was only teasing—after all, she didn't even know the real him—it was sort of heady to have Madison refer to him in that way.

He wondered idly how he would look with a tattoo. Just a small one, maybe, somewhere his patients wouldn't see. He'd discovered the tiny fairy on Madison's hip with both surprise and arousal, realizing it was positioned so that it could only be seen by those she chose to reveal it to. Preferring not to wonder how many others had admired that little drawing, he brushed a hand over her hip beneath the covers, savoring the silky feel of her.

"There's so much about you I don't know," he said.

Slowly stroking his arm with her left hand, she shrugged. "I'm a fourth-year psych resident, grew up and studied in Little Rock, except for attending college in Baton Rouge, Louisiana— where I met BiBi. Two older siblings, both surgeons, one widowed mother, no ex or current husbands, kids or pets. I'm applying for fellowships in several child and adolescent psych programs, so I'm not sure where I'll be this time next year. That pretty well tells you all there is to know."

It was actually quite a bit of information in a brief summary, but it wasn't nearly all he wanted to know about her. Dozens of questions swirled through his mind, with one taking priority. "Have you applied for a fellowship here in

Dallas? There's an excellent child psych program here, from what I've heard."

"Yes, I applied last month. I combined interviews with fittings for my bridesmaid's dress," she added with a laugh.

"Very efficient. So, um, how did the interview go? Did you like the program?" he asked, trying to sound only casually interested.

"I liked what I saw very much. And I think they liked me. I still have several interviews scheduled at other places before I rank my choices. I'm flying to Massachusetts and Oregon next week, so it'll be pretty hectic when I get back from the wedding. I've already interviewed in Indianapolis, Atlanta and Nashville."

Massachusetts. Oregon. Both a very long way from Dallas. "So you're not interested in staying closer to home?"

"I haven't decided yet. As close as I am to my family, it's tempting to consider living somewhere completely different for at least that one year."

Did she consider Dallas completely different than Little Rock?

"Somewhere more than a day's drive from home, maybe," she added. "The farthest I've lived from the house I grew up in was the seven-hour drive to Baton Rouge."

It wasn't even that far between Little Rock and Dallas. It was beginning to sound less likely that she would choose to pursue her fellowship here. He certainly didn't expect her to be influenced by a guy she'd known only a couple of days, and likely viewed as no more than a somewhat clandestine fling during a weekend away from her daily grind.

A "secret weekend adventure," she'd called it. At this point in her life, she didn't seem to be looking for more. Which meant he shouldn't waste one minute of the brief time he would have with her.

Sliding his hand from her hip to her bottom, he shifted closer to her, leaning over to brush her mouth with his. "Just how tired are you?" he asked in a murmur.

He was gratified when she moved her hand up his arm to his shoulder, her fingers curling to tug him even closer. "I'm wide-awake now," she assured him with a soft, somewhat breathless laugh.

"Good." He nipped at her lower lip, then started to settle onto her.

The buzz of a cell phone interrupted them just as she lifted her knees to welcome him.

Both of them grumbled in response to the ill-timed interruption, but their years of medical training made it impossible for either to simply ignore the summons. They reached simultaneously for their cell phones before Madison realized it wasn't her ring tone. Jason leaned over the side of the bed to scoop up his pants and dig his phone out of the pocket. He groaned when he checked the call screen.

"It's my youngest sister. Katie."

Madison glanced at the clock. It was almost midnight. "You'd better take it," she said, not even trying to hide her reluctance. "At this hour, something could be wrong."

He grimaced. "Katie's idea of a suitable time for phone calls is somewhat different than most people's. Not to mention her definition of a crisis."

Still, he lifted the phone to his ear, rolling to sit on the side of the bed as he answered. "What's up, Katie?"

It was impossible not to overhear his end of the conversation with him sitting inches away from her. Still, she didn't try to pay attention, merely closing her eyes and letting herself drift in a sensual haze, her limbs pleasantly heavy, her mouth curved in a soft smile.

She heard little snatches of his words.

"Can't you talk to Mom about…?"

"I'm sure Carly didn't mean…"

"If the two of you would just…"

He sighed heavily. "Okay, fine. I'll talk to Carly. Maybe I'll have a chance to call her sometime tomorrow between all this wedding stuff."

His voice sharpened only marginally when he spoke again. "I said I'll talk to her, Katie. Now I really have to go, okay? Good night."

Madison heard the buzz of an agitated feminine voice still coming through the phone when he disconnected the call. She opened her eyes. Jason pushed his free hand through his hair when he turned his head to look at her. "Sorry about that."

"Not a problem."

Perhaps he thought he should explain what he knew she'd overheard. "My sisters are squabbling. Again."

"And bringing you into it?"

He shrugged. "I'm used to it."

Her lips curved in response to the resigned look on his face. "The curse of being the firstborn," she said with a laugh. "I can't tell you how many times I turned to Meagan—my older sister—to solve problems for me. Especially when it was something I didn't necessarily want my parents to know about."

"The blessing of being the youngest," he quipped back.

She slid a hand up his arm and down again, fingertips tracing the muscles beneath his skin. "So, do you want to keep talking about family and careers and other mundane stuff? Or would you rather focus on us and the time we have left together?"

He tossed his phone aside and stretched out on the bed, reaching for her. "Us," he said firmly. "Definitely us."

Smiling in satisfaction, she wrapped her arms around his neck and snuggled closer to him. "Excellent choice."

"I really need to be going."

Though she hated to be reminded of anything

as mundane as passing time during this magical night, Madison glanced at the luminous red digits on the bedside clock. 2:00 a.m. She sighed reluctantly. "I suppose you should."

Propped on one elbow beside her, Jason stroked a strand of hair from her warm cheek. "I'll leave very discreetly. You won't have to worry about anyone seeing me slip out."

She laughed softly. "Now you sound like a P.I. Or a cat burglar."

Jason's chuckle rumbled in his chest. "Nah. My dad and some of my other relatives are the P.I.s. Usually—when I'm not seducing beautiful women in my role as a daring adventurer, of course—I'm just a simple family doc."

She was both flattered by being called beautiful, even teasingly, and intrigued by this new glimpse into his family, despite her reluctance earlier to talk about their real lives. "Seriously? Your dad is a private investigator?"

"BiBi didn't mention that, I take it?"

"I think I remember her talking about family friends who owned an investigation agency. I guess she meant your family."

"Yeah. My dad started the agency almost thirty years ago. Two of Mom's brothers joined him in it a couple years later. Now it's a fairly large investigation and security firm located here in Dallas with a branch in Houston. A few of my cousins work for Dee-Dub in various capacities, and my younger brother plans to work there as soon as he gets his bachelor's degree next year. He didn't actually want to go to college, hoping he could just go straight into the agency, but Mom and Dad insisted he get the degree first."

"Dee-Dub?" she repeated, wondering if she'd heard him correctly.

His lips twitched. "The D'Alessandro-Walker Agency. Dee-Dub for short, to the family."

"Ah. Sounds much less impressive that way."

He nodded. "Which is why we keep the nickname in the family."

"How did your dad feel about you going into medicine instead of following in his footsteps?"

Jason shrugged. "My folks have never really cared what careers we chose as long as we did our best in whatever field we entered. Laziness or mediocrity were not options in our family of overachievers."

"So you chose medicine on your own."

"It seemed to suit me. What about you?"

"I sort of followed my older siblings into it. Both of them are surgeons. I wouldn't say I was pressured into medicine, but it was strongly suggested as a practical and worthwhile career. So—I chose what some consider one of the least practical aspects of medicine. Psychiatry. Oddly enough, no one seemed startled by my choice."

"No one was surprised that I went into family practice, either," he admitted somewhat ruefully. "As Carly said, it was just the field a 'compulsive caregiver' like me would be expected to enter."

"A compulsive caregiver. Is that what you are?"

She knew that other people saw him that way;
was that the way he viewed himself?

"I guess," he said after a momentary hesitation.
"It seems to be a role I was born into."

"Do you ever feel like telling everyone to take
care of themselves and running off to do something wild and crazy?"

He laughed softly in response to her question.
"Often. But I know I won't. My life is here. My
heart is here with my family and my patients.
Guess I'm just not really the dashing, adventurous type."

"Oh, I don't know." She walked her fingers
up his chest, giving him a look from beneath
flirtatiously lowered lashes. "I'd say you were
fairly adventurous tonight."

He grinned and leaned down to kiss her. "Like
I've said, I'm different with you. And I've enjoyed every minute of it."

He seemed to view her as an anomaly in his
usual life—a vacation, of sorts, from the ex-

pectations of everyone else. She could live with that, she thought with a private smile. If Jason remembered her with fond smiles and maybe a little gratitude for the welcome break from his routines, she would consider their brief time together well spent.

There were many more things she would have liked to know about him. More details about his family, his practice, his hobbies, his plans and dreams for the future…but those were all the sort of questions that would come up between people who were getting to know each other with the possibility of continuing their relationship. The type of real-life information that would take some of the mystery and fantasy out of the time they'd spent together thus far and any discreet encounters they might have during the next two days, if opportunity presented itself. She suspected that Jason would prefer to leave those ordinary details unspoken, their whimsical charades intact.

"You should leave now, Dr. Jones," she murmured in "Esmeralda's" sultry voice. "It could be dangerous for you to be discovered here at sunrise."

His grin flashed white in the shadowy room, validating the choice she had made. "A kiss for luck before I go?"

Burying her fingers in his hair, she pulled his head down for a kiss that nearly singed the pillows beneath them. She felt his heart pounding against her when he lifted his head and said somewhat hoarsely, "Sunrise is still a few hours away."

As much as she would have liked for him to stay, she pressed her hands against his chest and gave a little push. They both needed rest if they were going to function coherently the next day. And besides, it really would be better if he slipped out without being seen. "Sorry. Time to go."

He sighed heavily, but reached for his clothes

without further procrastination. She tied her short robe loosely around her to walk him to the door so she could bolt the lock behind him. He stole one more kiss before opening the door, then drew a deep breath and glanced carefully out into the deserted hallway. "Sleep well," he whispered as he slipped out.

"Oh, I will," she assured him with a smile before closing the door and securing the lock.

She predicted very pleasant, if decidedly erotic dreams for what remained of that night.

What was left of the night passed all too quickly. Madison woke reluctantly when her cell phone alarm buzzed. As much as she would have loved to burrow into the Jason-scented pillows and snooze a while longer, she knew better than to be late for the bridesmaids' breakfast BiBi had scheduled to start this day. The breakfast would be followed by a visit to the hotel spa, a yoga class and a ladies' luncheon before the wedding rehearsal during the afternoon. After the rehearsal, two hours had been left free for everyone to change for a semiformal rehearsal dinner, followed by another dance, though this one would be much more genteel and sedate than the rowdy costume party Thursday night.

The groom's parents were hosting the postrehearsal festivities. BiBi had confided to Madison that it would probably be rather stuffy, but BiBi was leaving all the arrangements to her future mother-in-law for this part of the weekend, at least. No need to get off on the wrong foot with the woman even before the wedding, BiBi had added with a laugh. Very little about the day sounded like Madison's idea of fun. She'd never particularly enjoyed being pampered in a spa, wedding rehearsals were notoriously dull, formal dinners tended to be stilted and uncomfortable, and the dance would be equally awkward if her every move was watched by BiBi and Corinna whenever Jason was in the vicinity.

Reaching into the closet for the skirt and blouse she'd brought to wear to the breakfast, she shook her head. She would be changing at least three more times that day. She'd packed as light as she could, but BiBi's numerous plans had required a rather extensive wardrobe selection. It was no wonder she'd had no room to bring her own costume for the first night's party.

She spent a little extra time in the shower, letting the hot water soothe muscles that ached a bit from yesterday's activities—both daytime and nighttime. She didn't regret any of them. She hummed as she donned the red top and black-and-white-print skirt, then brushed her hair to a soft sheen. Suddenly realizing that she was humming "Bewitched, Bothered and Bewildered," she set down her brush and shook her head with a stern warning to herself. She had two more days to get through without upsetting BiBi and Corinna. Floating around with a sappy smile on her face and humming romantic songs was hardly the way to keep them from becoming suspicious.

Now if only she and Jason could pretend in front of the others that nothing had happened between them. She didn't like this feeling of slipping around, she thought as she tucked her key card into a small bag and headed for the elevator. Still, even if the awkward situation with Corinna hadn't been an issue, she would have chosen to keep her time with Jason private. It wasn't her style to flaunt her dalliances. All too familiar with wedding drama, she wouldn't have risked taking any of the spotlight off the bride with an open flirtation that would have been bound to stir gossip and speculation. But maybe she wouldn't have felt as much pressure to pretty much avoid Jason altogether when others were around.

That was going to be difficult.

BiBi stood at the door of the lovely glass-walled garden room where the bridesmaids' breakfast was being held a short while later. She greeted each of her friends with air kisses and hand squeezes. BiBi was smiling, but Madison thought she detected a faint edge of tension beneath her friend's deliberately cheery behavior. Was all the stress of the busy wedding weekend beginning to wear on BiBi? Madison had been concerned all along that BiBi had tried to cram too many activities into too few days.

BiBi's glossy lips brushed just over Madison's cheeks. "I can tell you slept well. You look rested and refreshed."

Thinking of the three hours or so of sleep she'd managed, Madison merely smiled. It wasn't sleep that had left her glowing this morning. "You look great, yourself. Love that top."

BiBi glanced down at the glittering, draped-neck blouse she wore with black pants. "You know I can never resist purple or sparkles."

"Well, it looks lovely on you. So, how are you holding up? Is everything going okay?"

BiBi hesitated only a moment before giving a little shrug. "There are a few last-minute complications in the arrangements. Things that shouldn't have cropped up because I've been planning and organizing everything for months, so you'd have thought everyone would know by now exactly what they're supposed to…"

She stopped and drew a deep breath, then shook her head in determination. "But I'm not going to worry about those things just now. First I'm going to enjoy this breakfast. Go, sit. They'll be serving mimosas in a few minutes and Corinna wants to start things off with a toast."

Because this was an intimate breakfast with only ten guests—the bride, her six bridesmaids, her mother and future mother-in-law, and the five-year-old flower girl, who was the daughter of one of the bridesmaids—one large, round table had been set to accommodate them.

Bouquets of white and deep purple roses decorated the center, sitting low enough to allow guests to see across the table. Silver place-card holders sat on the snowy tablecloth next to settings of fine white china and gleaming silverware. Madison was almost resigned to find that she was seated to the right of Corinna, whose mother, Tina Lovato, sat on Corinna's left.

Madison forced a big smile as she slipped into her chair, nodding to those already seated, who greeted her with smiles and a chorus of "good mornings." She was one of the last to arrive, even though she wasn't late.

She glanced to her left. "Good morning, Corinna."

"Good morning."

Madison couldn't tell any difference in Corinna's manner toward her, so if Corinna was still unsettled because Madison and Jason had delivered a baby together, she wasn't letting it show.

Might as well just get it out in the open. "Has anyone heard from Lila and Tommy this morning?"

"BiBi told me that Carl talked to Tommy first thing this morning," Corinna replied. "Tommy said to tell everyone that both Lila and the baby are doing well. They're going to stay another night in the hospital, then Tommy's taking them straight home to Houston. They'll miss the wedding, of course."

"It was ridiculous for them to come this weekend with a baby due so soon," Tina Lovato, mother of the bride, commented with a disapproving frown. "They're just lucky everything turned out well."

"Her baby wasn't actually due for another month," Deidre Burleson, mother of the groom, countered quickly, as if taking the other woman's words as a criticism of her son's choice of an usher. "They had no idea, of course, that the baby would come early, or I'm sure they never would have tried to be here."

"It still seems reckless to me," Tina insisted. "I know I never would have attempted a trip like that when I was expecting my girls. And now we're short an usher for the wedding."

Deidre shook her head insistently. "It's only a little over four hours' drive from here to Houston, not such a long trip. And Carl has already taken care of filling in Tommy's duties. Justin D'Alessandro—Jason's younger brother—is going to serve as an usher. He agreed this morning."

Seated beside Deidre, Hannah spoke up. "Lila was so fortunate to have not one, but two doctors to help deliver her baby. Madison and Jason worked so well together to take care of her."

Madison hoped the comment was innocently intended and not a deliberate attempt to stir a little friction between herself and Corinna. Madison was beginning to think Hannah rather enjoyed drama. To give Corinna credit, she merely nodded and said, "Yes, they did. Lila and Tommy were very grateful."

Madison shrugged self-deprecatingly. "We just did what we were trained to do in med school. I'm glad I was there to help. So, wasn't yesterday fun? I had a great time at the ranch. It's been ages since I was on horseback."

Angie Chen, a bridesmaid and friend of BiBi's from work, giggled. "The last time I was on horseback was a pony ride at a friend's tenth birthday party. I felt so awkward yesterday. But Corinna, you were great. I saw you win the barrel race. Wow."

Visibly pleased, Corinna smiled. "Thanks, Angie. I got lucky."

Toni Blanchard, Corinna's stiffest competition in the race, grumbled good naturedly. "She got lucky because I got a slower horse. If I'd had my Samson with me, you'd never have gotten near my time, Corinna."

"I'm sure you're right," Corinna agreed, then dimpled mischievously. "But then again, maybe I still would have won. I was in the zone yesterday."

"Brandon McCafferty certainly thought so," the final bridesmaid, Lucy Dixon, a cousin to BiBi and Corinna, remarked. "He couldn't take his eyes off you all day yesterday, you lucky girl. He's so cute."

A wave of pink touched Corinna's cheeks. "He is sort of cute," she admitted. "A little young for me, of course."

Lucy blew out a dismissive breath. "He's all of a few months younger than you. Not even a year, right? I know he was only a grade behind you back in school. He had a crush on you back then, too."

Corinna bit her lip for a moment, then reached determinedly for the glass of orange juice and champagne a server had just placed in front of her. She jumped to her feet. "Looks like everyone's here. BiBi, hang up the phone and come join your guests. Whatever glitch you're fretting about now can wait until after breakfast. I'm going to start things off with a toast."

Looking torn between irritation with the interruption and responsibility to her guests, BiBi disconnected the call she'd been on in one corner of the sunroom and hurried to her place at the table between her mother and mother-in-law-to-be.

"I was just talking to Jason," she admitted. "I wanted to tell him to make sure Justin's at the rehearsal later this afternoon. I know Carl's already given instructions, but I just wanted to make sure…"

"We're not talking about problems—or potential ones—now," Corinna cut in insistently. Some of the charming pink had left her cheeks now, and Madison didn't know whether to attribute it to her exasperation with her sister or the mention of Jason's name. Maybe a little of both, with emphasis on the latter.

As Corinna began a somewhat rambling toast to her older sister, Madison made a pretense of listening, her own mimosa in her hand in preparation for lifting it toward the bride. She found her thoughts drifting backward a few hours, to a perfect, intimate moment in Jason's arms. A flood of warmth filled her in response to the thought, making her moisten her lips and long for the cool drink waiting in her hand.

She wondered if Jason was listening to a wordy toast at the groomsmen's breakfast, thinking of her and remembering a few perfect moments.

She couldn't help wondering somewhat wistfully if she would ever know that sort of perfection again. At that moment, she couldn't imagine discovering such ecstasy with anyone but Jason. That unwelcome thought was enough to make her gulp her mimosa a bit too urgently when the toast ended, causing her to cough and sputter into her napkin.

Both BiBi and Corinna looked at her oddly, but she kept her expression bland, commenting lightly that the drink had gone down the wrong way. If she was going to get through the next day and a half without any repercussions to her friendship with BiBi, she was going to have to make a concerted effort not to think about Jason at all.

That would definitely not be easy, she thought, taking another, more careful sip of her drink before reaching for her fork with a bright smile for her table mates.

Chapter Seven

BiBi's wedding planner had the personality of a hardened drill sergeant, Madison decided later that afternoon. Her name was Phyllis Crumble and her round, pink face was deceptively innocuous. She gave instructions in a sweetly musical voice, but the moment someone stepped out of line, she barked corrections in a firm, don't-mess-with-me tone that would have made any schoolteacher proud. Even BiBi seemed a bit intimidated by the woman she had hired to ensure the wedding went smoothly.

Phyllis worked with the ushers first, giving them instructions and then insisting that each one escort her down the aisle, and woe to them if they didn't ask, "Bride's side or groom's side?"

Madison had to hide a smile when young Justin D'Alessandro gave his brother a harried, what-did-I-get-myself-into look after his training session. Apparently, he'd accidentally escorted Phyllis to the wrong side of the church when she'd asked to sit on the groom's side, and he'd been sternly reprimanded. And then Phyllis patted his cheek and told him he'd done a wonderful job before she turned to the next nervous usher.

If it took this long just to drill the ushers, Madison couldn't help wondering how long it would take until Phyllis was satisfied with the rest of the wedding party's performances. It had already been a rather long day, and it was far from over.

Though the time in the spa had been intended

to be relaxing, it hadn't been overly successful, as far as Madison was concerned. BiBi seemed to be growing more stressed as the wedding drew nearer, which rather surprised Madison. BiBi had seemed so blissfully happy when the long weekend began. Madison couldn't imagine that her friend was getting cold feet about the marriage itself, so she wasn't sure why BiBi was being so obsessive about the wedding details. Every little glitch sent her into another frenzy of phone calls and pacing, and glitches were inevitable with plans as detailed as BiBi's. While it hadn't surprised Madison at all that BiBi was being such a perfectionist this weekend, she had thought her friend would handle the setbacks better than she had thus far.

Madison had been waiting for a chance to speak to BiBi in private, but that opportunity hadn't yet presented itself. Either BiBi had been surrounded by other people in the spa or at the luncheon following, or she'd been on the phone or in a frantic discussion with her mother or wedding planner. Now that rehearsals were underway in the church only a few blocks from the hotel, there was certainly no way to pull BiBi aside.

As directed by the wedding planner, Madison stood at the back of the church with the other bridesmaids, mothers of the bride and groom, and the flower girl and ring bearer while the ushers were being trained. Carl and his groomsmen were grouped at the front of the church waiting to be herded to the side room where they would listen for their cue in the ceremony.

"That will do," Phyllis finally pronounced. She made a note in her ever-present notebook, dismissing the ushers. Justin and the other three ushers quickly escaped to sit in a tight clump on a pew at the back side of the church where they seemed to hope she couldn't see them.

Phyllis raised her voice so that everyone in the church could hear her clearly. For a small woman, she projected very well. "Once the guests are seated, the soloist will perform before the grandmothers and mothers are escorted into the church."

"Maybe I should have chosen that other song I was considering," BiBi fretted from behind Madison. "What do you think, Mother? Should I have Lorelei sing them both for me again? She said she would be happy to sing either."

"She didn't say it was okay for you to change your mind twenty-four hours before the wedding," Corinna countered. "She and the pianist have already practiced several times. That song will be fine."

"I think that's my decision, not yours," BiBi snapped.

Madison knew that tone. Her friend was on the verge of a hissy fit. BiBi didn't let her temper get out of control often, but when she did…well, suffice it to say that was one reason Madison had been so cautious that weekend. She loved

BiBi, knew her to be a loving, generous, warm-hearted woman, but she had learned years earlier to avoid BiBi in full-on diva mode.

"The song is beautiful, BiBi," their mother interceded swiftly, also familiar with her older daughter's sometimes capricious moods. "And you said it was special to you and Carl. I think you should keep it."

BiBi nodded shortly. "Fine. We'll keep it."

"Is there a problem back there?" Phyllis inquired, looking up from her notebook, obviously displeased at not having everyone's full attention.

"No problem," Tina replied cheerily. "Carry on."

"Thank you." Phyllis cleared her throat. "After the soloist performs…"

"I heard she used to teach junior high before switching to wedding planning," Hannah murmured to Madison.

Madison stifled a laugh. "That doesn't surprise me at all," she whispered back.

She stood back and watched as Phyllis sent the groom and his attendants to the side room. "Listen for your cue, now," she warned them. "We'll practice your entrance a couple of times before the bridesmaids rehearse."

Carl and his friends turned obediently to obey her instructions. Jason glanced casually toward the back of the church as he filed out, and Madison spun quickly away before their eyes could meet. She'd had little chance to interact with him that day. They'd sat at different tables during lunch and had arrived separately at the church for the rehearsal. Yet she had been acutely aware of him whenever they'd been in the same room, even if they were facing opposite directions. He'd been equally careful not to give any indication that he noticed her, but she suspected he was aware of her, too. How could they not be focused on each other, considering the connection they had formed during the night together?

She looked toward the ushers, noticing that Corinna had slipped over there and was now giggling animatedly, if very quietly, with Brandon McCafferty. Corinna had to be flattered by the fascination on Brandon's face when he looked at her. He seemed to be enthralled by her every word and gesture, and what woman wouldn't respond to that, especially when another man had recently made it clear that he wasn't enchanted by her?

Madison was pretty sure there was a new appreciation in Corinna's eyes for Brandon, who really was a very attractive man. Not as gorgeous as Jason—but then, not many men were, she thought with a ripple of wry exasperation with herself.

She hoped Corinna and Brandon hit it off—not because Madison wanted Jason for herself, but because Corinna deserved to give her heart to someone who wanted it, and who was eager to give his own in return. Whatever suspicions Corinna might have had about Madison earlier had seemed to fade during the day. She had been relaxed during the spa time and lunch, as polite as ever toward Madison. Either she had convinced herself that nothing was going on between Madison and Jason, or she'd decided to move on from her unrequited crush. Whatever the reason, Madison was relieved, and even more convinced that discretion had definitely been the right decision for herself and Jason.

Madison noticed that BiBi was nearby and for once not talking on her phone or conversing with anyone else. Madison took advantage of the opportunity to ask, "How are you holding up, Beebs? Getting a little stressed?"

"Why? Are you saying I look stressed?" BiBi frowned and whirled to study her image in a gilt-framed mirror on the foyer wall. "Oh, damn, I look terrible. Bags under my eyes, and my skin looks yellow."

Everyone within range of her plaintive complaint hastened to assure her that she looked as beautiful as ever. Fluttering around her daughter anxiously, Tina shot Madison a look of reproof, as if Madison had deliberately upset the anxious bride.

Madison sighed, losing patience. "BiBi, could I talk to you for a minute?"

"There's no time for a talk now," Tina said, tapping her watch. "Phyllis is going to want to start rehearsal for the procession as soon as the men know their places. And we don't want to annoy Phyllis."

Everyone nodded as if that were a given.

"Excuse me." Phyllis spoke loudly enough to draw all attention to herself as she faced the front of the church. "Where is the third groomsman?" She glanced at her notebook. "Jason D'Alessandro?"

Madison followed Phyllis's disapproving glare. Carl stood in place in front of the altar, flanked by his best man, his older brother, Curtis. Their cousin Allen stood beside Curtis, and there was an obvious gap between Allen and the remaining three groomsmen.

Carl cleared his throat. "Umm, Jason's on the phone. A call from a patient."

Phyllis crossed her arms. "We'll wait."

Carl shook his head. "He warned it could take a while. He said he's been a groomsman before, so he knows what to do."

"Seriously?" BiBi threw up her hands. "Jason's blowing off the rehearsal? I cannot believe this."

"He's not blowing it off," Carl argued, dividing his wary attention between his fiancé and the wedding planner. "He's a doctor. He had to take the call."

"He's off duty," BiBi snapped back. "And he has partners who are supposed to be covering for him. If he couldn't take time off for our wedding, he shouldn't have agreed to be a groomsman."

Justin started to rise from his seat with the other ushers. "Jason wouldn't interrupt everything with a call unless it was important," he insisted loyally. "You know he takes his responsibilities seriously—to his patients and to the commitments he makes to his friends."

Phyllis clapped her hands imperiously. "We must move on," she said firmly. "I'll have to trust that the rest of you men will direct Jason into position when the time comes. Now, we must line up the processional, flower girl and ring bearer first, followed by the bridesmaids in the following order."

Consulting her notebook, she barked names and each attendant moved quickly into position. Madison found herself standing between Hannah and Lucy. Corinna followed Lucy, after which BiBi would enter. Which made Madison the third bridesmaid. She would be walking out of the church with Jason, she realized abruptly. She didn't know whether to be more pleased by the coincidence or concerned about the potential awkwardness.

She could still hear BiBi muttering behind her when the music started and they prepared to begin their evenly paced walk up the aisle. Over to the side, Justin still glowered in response to the criticism of his brother. Madison hoped the call was really important enough to warrant this tension. As unreasonable as BiBi had been at times that day, Madison could almost agree with her on this point. After all, Madison was also a doctor, and yet she allowed herself to turn off her phone occasionally when she was away from work. Even physicians were allowed to have a personal life, though not all of their patients always agreed with that sentiment.

Remembering BiBi's comments about the complaints Jason's last girlfriend had made about his overdeveloped commitment to his family and his practice, Madison told herself it was just as well she wasn't expecting anything from him after this random weekend. From the day she'd entered medical school, she had vowed that her career would not completely rule her life, and she couldn't imagine trying to have a relationship with someone who did live that way. Since Jason hadn't made any big changes to salvage his relationship with his ex, either he liked his life exactly the way it was, or he didn't want to add yet another commitment to his already demanding schedule.

Their wedding weekend fling must have been as relaxingly appealing for him as it was to her, she mused, pretending to hold a bouquet as she responded to a nod from Phyllis and began the measured walk up the aisle. Enjoy, have fun, then walk away unscathed and unfettered. Whatever Jason's motivations, this was entirely the wrong time for her to add complications to her own life. Including, she thought with a glance over her shoulder, a clash with her longtime friend.

Phyllis ran them through the procession twice before she was satisfied. Once everyone was in place at the front of the church, she studied them critically before giving a nod. "Fine. Now, let's rehearse the walk out. Bride and groom, you will turn toward your guests while the minister presents you as a married couple. Bride, retrieve your bouquet from your maid of honor…"

Corinna pretended to pass invisible flowers to her sister, who smiled a bit tightly.

"…and you begin your walk down the aisle, followed by the ring bearer and flower girl. Micah, offer your arm to Nicole the way I showed you earlier. Yes, that's lovely. Now, follow the bride and groom to the exit. Not too fast. All right, best man, offer your arm to the maid of honor. Now, next couple. And the third…oh, dear. Well, Madison, you'll just have to pretend."

Stifling a wry smile, Madison fell into step

behind Lucy and Allen. It wasn't hard to pretend that Jason was at her side. She could imagine him next to her in a variety of interesting poses. With only a bit more effort, she could almost feel him touching her again, making her pulse race in a manner that was probably unbecoming for a bridesmaid.

Jason waited for them in the church foyer, his expression penitent as he stepped toward BiBi. "I'm very sorry, BiBi. If the call hadn't been important, I never would have…"

"It's okay, Jason," Carl said hastily. "It's not like it's hard to just walk out and stand there, especially since you've done this before."

BiBi gave her fiancé a stern look. "Well, since you find everything so easy, there was really no reason for us to rehearse at all, was there?"

"Now, honey…"

"BiBi, I'm really sorry…"

BiBi shook her head at both men, drew a deep breath, then turned determinedly toward her wedding planner. "Was that rehearsal sufficient, Phyllis, or should we run through it all again now that everyone has joined us?"

Jason winced, and everyone else, like Madison, seemed to hold their breath, hoping Phyllis would call it enough. The flower girl was beginning to whine a little, plaintively informing her mother that she was hungry. The planner seemed tempted to begin again, but a glance at her watch had her shaking her head. "No, that will do."

After a collective sigh of relief, the members of the wedding party began to gather their things in preparation for leaving the church. There was still a formal rehearsal dinner to be followed by the groom's family's gala, which meant yet another change of clothing.

Madison was beginning to wonder if BiBi would make it through the remainder of the day without suffering a meltdown. What on earth was going on with her friend? She'd seemed fine yesterday.

As the church cleared, Madison couldn't help noticing that Corinna frowned at Jason before turning to be escorted from the church by Brandon. Was Corinna, too, irked with Jason about missing rehearsal? Maybe she was beginning to agree with his ex-girlfriend that as good-looking and charming as he was, it took too much effort to compete with all the other obligations in his life. Especially when Corinna had totally attentive Brandon there to compare to Jason.

Jason walked beside Madison as they descended the stairs to the sidewalk outside the church. Some of the wedding party had come in their own cars. Because it was such a beautiful day, Madison and a few others who were staying at the hotel had walked the few blocks to the rehearsal. Jason and his brother had already been at the church when she'd arrived.

"I think I'm in trouble," Jason murmured, his tone both regretful and resigned.

"I don't think you're on BiBi's list of favorite people at the moment," Madison agreed.

"I know the timing was bad, but I had to take the call. One of my patients needed to consult with me, and I had to make another related call after I talked to her."

"Your patients have your personal cell number? Don't your partners handle your calls for you when you're not in the office?"

"This patient is a longtime friend of the family. Mom gave her my number. It's a long story."

"And one that's not at all my business," she said breezily, stepping down onto the sidewalk.

Justin met them there. Tall and dark, he looked so much like a younger version of Jason that Madison couldn't help simply admiring the attractive pair for a moment. Justin wore his near-black hair longer and more casually than Jason's, and his face hadn't quite lost the softness of youth to mature into Jason's more chiseled features, but the resemblance really was striking.

"My car's in the side parking lot," Justin informed his brother. "Want a ride back to the hotel? I want you to hear my new speakers."

"Sure. As long as you don't blow out my eardrums."

Justin grinned. "Well, darn. Take all the fun out of it, why don't you?"

Jason turned to Madison, speaking casually as he introduced his younger brother. "Would you like a ride back? I'm relatively sure the kid can get us there in one piece."

She smiled, but shook her head. "Thank you, but I'll walk. It's such a nice day, and this is my only chance to get any sunshine before the dinner and dance this evening."

Jason groaned. "I've got to say, I'm getting a little partied out."

"Why do I have the feeling tonight's going to be really dull?" Justin asked in a low voice.

"Because it will be," Jason answered bluntly.

"Anytime the invitation says 'semiformal,' you can bet the party will be a snoozer."

Justin groaned. "Like Mom's fundraisers we're always trying to find excuses to miss?"

"You got it."

"Maybe the ushers aren't really expected to attend," Justin said hopefully. "I mean, BiBi said she'd see me at the rehearsal dinner, but maybe she wouldn't even notice if I…"

Jason shook his head. "Forget it, bro. I'm already in the doghouse with BiBi. Don't you get the whole family on her bad side. She considers herself doing you the honor of allowing you to be an usher and attend this dinner thing. You'd better show up."

While Justin sighed in surrender, Madison glanced toward the church entrance. Speaking of BiBi…

"I'd better go," she said, addressing both brothers. "I need to change before dinner. Wouldn't want to be late."

Following her glance, Jason must have seen BiBi watching them. His eyes narrowed a bit and his voice was just a little clipped when he said, "I could walk with you."

Already moving away, she shook her head. "Justin wants you to hear his speakers. See you guys later."

With an airy wave toward both of them, she turned and strode rapidly away, catching up with Hannah and Lucy, who were also strolling toward the hotel. Surely BiBi wouldn't fault her for chatting with the D'Alessandro brothers on the way out of the church. If so, she was going to have a find time for a long talk with her. As it was, she hoped to find time to chat with BiBi in private that evening. She'd like to know what was bothering her friend, and if there was anything she could do to help.

Whether she would have a chance to talk with Jason in private again—well, that remained to be seen.

* * *

Justin didn't drive straight to the hotel. The brothers had decided there was time for a quick cup of coffee before they had to prepare for the evening, so they stopped at a nearby coffee shop, where Jason ordered espresso and Justin chose a cappuccino and a monster-size chocolate chip cookie.

"She's pretty," Justin commented around a mouthful of cookie.

Drawn from his thoughts, Jason looked up from his cup. "What? Who?"

"Madison Baker. The bridesmaid you couldn't stop staring at. She's pretty."

"I wasn't staring at her." He hadn't been, had he? Was that part of the reason BiBi had been giving him the evil eye for missing a portion of the rehearsal?

"Okay, maybe you weren't staring, but I could tell you like her."

"You've got foam on your lip."

It was a poor excuse for a distraction and Justin didn't fall for it. He swiped a paper napkin across his mouth before persisting. "Are you going to ask her out?"

"No."

"How come?"

"She lives in Arkansas. She's headed back there after the wedding."

"Oh." Justin nodded as if that settled the question. "Bummer."

"I guess." Jason wondered if he and Madison would have gotten together if she hadn't lived in another state. As beautifully as they had meshed this weekend, they'd both known it was only temporary. Did they have enough in common that temporary could have become permanent? He supposed he would never know the answer to that.

"Katie said Aunt Tina's ticked off with you because you wouldn't go out with Corinna. Katie said the families have been hoping the two of you would get together since you were kids."

"Bull. They tried for years to hook me up with BiBi, even pressured me to ask her to the prom. Fortunately, she was never interested. She was crazy about Carl even back then, though they broke up for a few years before getting back together. It wasn't until they gave up on BiBi and me that they decided to throw Corinna at me as a default," he said bluntly.

Tina Lovato wasn't actually their aunt, of course, just a longtime family friend. But the fact that she felt like an aunt to them went a long way toward explaining why Jason couldn't even imagine dating either BiBi or Corinna, any more than he'd have asked out one of his Walker or D'Alessandro cousins. Maybe they weren't actually blood kin, but they might as well have been, considering how long they'd known each other. There was just no mystery, no chemistry, no…

No *adventure,* he thought, the word making him think of Madison again, for some reason.

"I had a thing for Corinna once," Justin mused, breaking off another piece of cookie. "I think I was twelve and she was about fifteen. I was just starting to notice girls and she...well, she was definitely a girl."

Jason chuckled, remembering the way Brandon had stared at Corinna when she'd ridden the mechanical bull. Brandon had been in danger of swallowing his Adam's apple.

Considering the looks Corinna had given Jason that afternoon, he thought it was safe to say that her infatuation with him was over, whether or not she returned Brandon's interest. And that was fine by him; he just hoped that someday, hopefully sooner than later, they could get back onto the easy "old friend" footing he shared with BiBi. Or had shared with BiBi, until an inconveniently timed telephone call had made her look at him as if he'd deliberately tried to sabotage her fairy-tale wedding.

He was getting a bit tired of trying to keep the Lovato family happy this weekend. He understood bridal jitters, having seen enough of them in his own extended family. But, damn.

His phone beeped. He glanced at it automatically. "Carly."

"Wonder what she wants from you now?"

"What makes you think she wants something?"

Justin gave him a look.

Jason sighed and lifted the phone to his ear, conceding the point. "Hey, sis. What's up?"

Madison finally caught up with BiBi later that evening. During the elegant meal set up in a glittering hotel dining room, BiBi had sat at the table of honor, along with her fiancé, their parents and siblings. Seated at another table with several of the bridesmaids and their spouses, Madison had kept an eye on BiBi while they'd dined to the

sounds of quiet conversation, clinking silverware and suitably subdued music from a string
quartet set up in one corner of the room. BiBi
had seemed to enjoy the meal. She'd smiled and
even laughed several times, making the others
at the table with her look a bit more relaxed than
they had earlier when she'd been so stressed.

And yet...

During the past ten years, Madison had seen
BiBi in almost every mood, and she could sense
that something still wasn't quite right. So, when
BiBi slipped into the restroom while desserts
were being served, Madison followed.

BiBi was studying her reflection in the mirror,
an uncapped tube of lipstick in one hand.

"You look beautiful, as always," Madison assured her with a smile, leaning one hip against
the counter to study her friend. She'd spoken
the truth. With her dark hair swept into a pretty
twist and her curvy figure nicely displayed in
a jewel-toned silk dress, BiBi had never looked

better. Madison had worn a simple black sleeve-less sheath chosen both for its flattering cut and wrinkle-resistance. She had dressed it up with a glint of diamonds at her ears and throat and high-heeled strappy sandals.

"I think I've gained weight this weekend," BiBi fretted. "Too many desserts."

"Don't be silly, you don't look as though you've gained an ounce. Besides, it's your special week-end. Enjoy the sweets and diet later."

"Easy for you to say. You never have to worry about your weight."

"The closer I get to thirty, the harder I have to work to burn the calories," Madison said with a shrug.

BiBi muttered something indistinguishable and touched up her lipstick. Madison pulled her lip gloss out of her tiny bag and leaned slightly toward the mirror, speaking casually as she out-lined her lips. "Everything has gone remarkably smoothly this weekend. Everyone seems to be having a nice time. You must be pleased."

"I guess. I didn't expect so many problems to crop up last minute. I thought I'd planned for everything."

"You couldn't have planned for everything," Madison said logically. "You certainly couldn't predict Lila would go into labor early, for example."

"Or that Jason would go AWOL during the rehearsal. Could you believe that?"

"I can see why you'd be irritated," Madison responded carefully.

BiBi shot her a narrow look. "You're not going to leap to his defense? Heaven knows everyone else has, except Corinna, who was almost as mad as I was. Mom told me I was being unreasonable. She kept saying Jason's a doctor, like that makes him so much more important than everyone else."

"Obviously, I don't agree with that sentiment.

And I think you have every right to be annoyed by the interruption."

"Jason's just been sort of a jerk this weekend. Thinks he's too good for Corinna, and apparently too important to have to rehearse for my wedding."

Madison thought that was a bit too harsh, but she knew better than to argue Jason's case just then. It wasn't her place to do so, anyway. He'd have to find his own way of making amends with BiBi.

Shoving her lipstick into her bag, BiBi muttered, "Nothing to say? You seemed pretty impressed by him earlier."

Madison turned and crossed her arms over her chest. "Is there something you want to get off your chest, Beebs? I want you to enjoy the rest of your weekend, and I'm not sure you can do that if you're stewing about something."

"Don't go all shrink on me, Maddie. Not tonight."

"I'm not speaking as a shrink, but as your friend. You've seemed tense all day. If there's anything I can do to help…"

BiBi spun to face her. "Do you think my wedding weekend is pretentious and overdone?"

"What? No, of course I don't. Why would you think I—"

BiBi held up a hand. "It wasn't you. I heard these women…"

She stopped and drew a quick breath, then began again. "This morning, I was awake really early. Too wired to sleep. So I slipped down to the lobby coffee shop for a latte. I was sitting at a little corner table going over my lists for today and tomorrow when I heard a couple of women talking on the other side of a stained-glass divider. They didn't know I was there, I guess, but they were saying my weekend has been pretentious and overdone. They were speculating about how much we've paid for everything, and saying we're flashing our cash and wasting good money."

"That's absurd, BiBi. You and Carl have been saving for this wedding for more than a year. And no one who knows you would ever call you pretentious." Which was the absolute truth. Carl and BiBi both came from financially comfortable families, and Carl, at least, was making good money now, but BiBi wasn't the type to flaunt her good fortune. She preferred sharing it. As much as BiBi had enjoyed being the center of attention this weekend, the intention behind all her plans was to make sure her guests had a good time, and that they would remember how much fun her wedding had been.

"I know, right? We've been saving like crazy. And we aren't even paying for everything. The costume party was thrown by our friends, the luncheons were hosted by other people, everything this evening is on Carl's parents."

Madison waved off the litany, having little interest in who was funding what. "These women you heard. Did you recognize their voices?"

"No. I don't even think they're guests of the wedding. I think they're staying at the hotel and they've been hearing about the festivities through gossip. They seemed familiar with Carl's family by reputation, but I don't think they know them well, if at all."

"Then why are you obsessing about this?" Madison asked in genuine bafflement. "A couple of women you don't even know were being catty, and you're letting it ruin your wedding weekend?"

"It's not ruining…I mean, you have to admit a lot of things have gone wrong. Despite all the saving and planning, I can't help wondering if maybe I got carried away and tried to do too much. And I can't help wondering if other people are thinking the same thing as those women, but are being too polite to tell me."

"From what I've seen, your guests are having a great time. I know I have been."

BiBi sighed. "Thanks, Maddie. I can always count on you to cheer me up. Even though I've been such a jerk to you. I can't believe I brought up Steve Gleason. I'm sorry about that."

Madison was still a bit irked by that, but now wasn't the time to say so. "You know you can always talk to me," she said instead.

Glancing toward the door, BiBi wrinkled her nose. "I should probably get back to my guests."

"Your mom will come looking for you soon," Madison agreed.

"So, you're sure you don't want to get to know Allen better?" BiBi asked with a smile that was both teasing and resigned. "If you married him, we could be cousins-in-law."

"Or I could not marry him and we could just stay very good friends," Madison countered fondly.

BiBi linked her arm with Madison's as they

left the restroom. "Funny. I was sure you and Allen would hit it off. You have so much in common."

Madison couldn't imagine what common ground BiBi imagined between her and Allen, but she merely shrugged. "Guess I'm just not in the right place for anything serious right now."

"Well, if you ever are in that place, give me a call. Maybe I'll have someone else picked out for you by then," BiBi said with a short laugh. "And in the meantime, I'm still going to try to talk you into coming to Dallas for your fellowship. I would so love living that close to you again."

Madison forced a noncommittal smile. Something told her that no matter how long it would be until she made that unlikely call, she knew who BiBi would *not* choose for her.

As for whether she would choose to move to Dallas for her fellowship…well, for some reason that choice suddenly seemed much more complicated.

Chapter Eight

The guests who attended the dance after dinner Saturday evening were considerably more dignified than the ones who'd partied so avidly at the Thursday night masquerade. For one thing, the average age of these guests, all invited by the groom's parents, was older than the contemporaries of the engaged couple who'd thrown the costume party. The alcohol consumption was less conspicuous and the music much more sedate. Even the clothing had much to do with the difference in tone. Masks and costumes had encouraged people to shed some of their usual inhibitions and social decorum, whereas tonight they were on their best behavior in their party dresses and tailored suits.

Madison found herself talking shop quite a bit during the event, as several other physicians were in attendance. She never introduced herself as Dr. Baker, but the mothers of the bride and groom insisted on adding the title whenever they presented her to another guest. That inevitably led to talk of work and her plans for the future.

She'd found that people not in the medical field had either little or incorrect knowledge of psychiatry and mental illness. Some had a little trouble understanding that yes, a psychiatrist was a medical doctor, a fully trained physician. Many didn't know the difference between psychiatry and psychology, having been misled by unrealistic portrayals in books, on TV and in movies. Those same media often grossly misrepresented people suffering from mental illnesses, the majority of whom would never be a danger to others. She was also accustomed to people sometimes withdrawing from her when they found out she was a "shrink," as if in concern that she might analyze them and find them lacking in some way. Not to mention those who had to tell her all about their crazy relatives or acquaintances.

From the few snatches of Jason's conversations she caught by accident during the evening, she knew he, too, spent at least part of the evening talking about work. As a family physician, he was hit up frequently for free medical advice. She didn't get that quite as much as he did. More people were willing to discuss their physical ailments than any possible psychological issues, at least where they, themselves, were concerned. While she was sure Jason knew how to gracefully deflect those inquiries, he seemed to spend more time with them than she would be inclined to do.

The dance floor wasn't nearly as crowded for this dance as it had been at the costume party. Still, a few men asked Madison to dance, and she accepted. Carl, his brother, BiBi's dad, a podiatrist introduced to her by BiBi's mom, a couple of others. Allen notably did not ask, spending most of his time near Hannah. So much for BiBi's matchmaking scheme that weekend.

She was helping herself to a glass of champagne punch when Jason finally approached her. He did so very casually, plucking a chocolate-dipped strawberry off the snack table near where she stood as if that had been his primary intention. "Having a good time?"

"Yes, lovely, thanks. And you?"

"It's a nice party."

So courteous and impersonal. She doubted anyone overhearing would suspect that she knew exactly what lay beneath Jason's beautifully tailored dark suit, exactly how it felt to run her hands over the sleek chest hidden beneath his snowy-white shirt and deep red tie.

"So, how about it? Want to take a spin around the dance floor?"

She had hoped he wouldn't ask. Maybe he thought it would look odder if he didn't. She kept her smile friendly, suitably vague. "Thank you, but I believe I'll take a break with this drink. It feels as though I've been on my feet all day. I'll see you later, Jason."

His eyes narrowed, but she turned away before he could respond. As she crossed the room, she remembered his expression. He had not liked her rejection, as polite as she'd tried to be about it. She wasn't sure if she'd hurt his ego or his feelings, but either way, she still thought she'd made the right call.

Probably no one would lift an eyebrow at the sight of her dancing with Jason, no more than they had when she'd danced with Carl or Curtis or the others she'd danced with so casually during the past couple of hours. No one, that is, except the Lovato sisters. Corinna, of course, probably noticed whenever Jason danced with anyone else, even though she'd missed few opportunities to take to the dance floor, herself. She had partnered with several of the male guests, and Brandon had hovered near her all evening to fill in the gaps.

As for BiBi, she had already homed in on the undercurrents between Madison and Jason. Even if she didn't know exactly what was going on, she knew Madison well enough to sense something…enough that it had brought back those uncomfortable memories from college. Madison wasn't sure she could dance with Jason, no matter how circumspectly, without once again triggering BiBi's intuition where her longtime friend was concerned.

Maybe she would have a chance to explain that to Jason later. Not that she owed him explanations, of course. She was under no obligation to dance with him this evening, no matter what had happened between them last night. After tomorrow, there was a good chance she would never even see him again.

She tried to fill the faint hollowness left by that thought with several long swallows of her punch.

She really wasn't expecting Jason to follow when she slipped out into the garden a short while later. The last time she had seen him, he'd appeared to be making his way toward the exit, stopping to chat with acquaintances along the way. It was getting late, and he wouldn't be the first guest to leave. She didn't plan to stay much longer, herself. After getting a quick breath of fresh air, she would find BiBi and say good-night. Tomorrow was the big day, and they both needed rest.

Sitting on one of the little benches, she closed her eyes for a moment. The autumn air was cool against her cheeks and bare arms, hinting

at colder weather ahead. The sound of the fountain in the center of the small courtyard was so
soothing that she fancied she could drift off to
sleep if she sat there much longer. With a faint
sigh, she opened her eyes.

Jason stood in front of her, his arms crossed
over his chest, a look of exaggerated patience on
his face as he waited for her to notice him. To
give her credit, she didn't jump, though she did
blink a few times in her surprise at seeing him.
"I thought you'd left already."

"I was on my way to the exit when I saw you
slip out here."

She glanced automatically toward the doorway.

His mouth twisted. "Don't worry, I made sure
to be discreet when I came out. I doubt anyone
knows we're out here together, actually exchanging words with each other."

He was definitely aggravated with her. Seemed

like whatever she did that weekend, someone ended up irritated.

She sighed and pushed a hand through her hair. "You know why I turned down your invitation to dance, Jason. I just didn't want to call any attention to us."

"You've danced several times with other people. I've been on the dance floor once or twice, myself. I wouldn't think anyone would find it the least odd that I would ask you to dance with me, considering we'll be walking down the aisle together tomorrow."

"Oh, so someone filled you in on your responsibilities for tomorrow?" she asked before she could stop herself.

His eyebrows rose. His response was equally blunt. "That was a bit cattier than I would have expected from you."

"Sorry," she said, though she wasn't particularly. She was getting tired of walking on eggshells this weekend. Around BiBi and Corinna and Jason, too, for that matter.

Looking aggrieved, he said rather curtly, "I've apologized to everyone for missing some of the rehearsal this afternoon."

"Some of the rehearsal?" she repeated. "You missed all your own part."

"I think I can handle walking unrehearsed," he shot back. "And I'm getting tired of groveling because I had to take a call."

She held up a hand. "You're right. You certainly don't owe me any apologies or explanations. BiBi's the one who was upset."

"I'm getting damned tired of tiptoeing around BiBi, too," he snapped, far from mollified. "I know it's her weekend, and I understand bridal jitters and such, but come on. Refusing to dance with me because it might anger BiBi because it just might upset Corinna, to whom I have absolutely no obligation and who looks quite happy dancing with Brandon McCafferty anyway? That's carrying things a little too far, don't you think?"

"You don't understand."

"You're right. I *don't* understand. It was just a dance."

"And maybe it wouldn't have caused any problems at all. I just wasn't willing to take that risk."

She sensed him withdraw even more into himself. Surely he understood that she had to put BiBi's feelings ahead of his, considering that she had known him only a few days.

He took a step backward, his expression shuttered. With his new position, the shadow of a potted palm tree fell over the upper half of his face, so that only the glitter of his dark eyes and the hard set of his mouth were visible to her. "I won't put you at any further risk of being seen with me. Good night, Madison. I'll see you at the ceremony tomorrow."

She groaned. "Jason—"

He turned and walked away without giving her another chance to…what? Apologize again? Explain again?

"Oh, forget it," she muttered, jumping to her feet. She started toward the ballroom, then made herself pause a few minutes so she wouldn't be seen entering immediately after him.

Okay, maybe her exaggerated caution was sort of silly. Maybe he was right that she was worrying a bit too much about BiBi's overwrought sensibilities. It would be hard for any guy to understand the complicated history she and BiBi shared. But whether justified or not, it was entirely her decision how much she wanted to cater to her friend.

Deciding enough time had passed, she entered the ballroom and headed straight for BiBi. She would say her good-nights and then go up to her room. She was suddenly very tired. She only hoped she would be able to sleep in the bed that now held too many disconcerting memories.

Though she wasn't yet asleep, she had already crawled between the sheets when a quiet knock came on her door. Having no doubt who stood on the other side, she hesitated a moment before swinging her legs over the edge of the bed. She knew he would take the hint and go away if she didn't answer. But she crossed the room anyway, and it wasn't only because she didn't want anyone to see him standing outside her door.

She hadn't bothered with a robe, but he'd seen her in less than the short emerald satin chemise she now wore. She opened the door and motioned him inside.

As he had the night before, he'd changed before coming to her room. His dark suit had been replaced by a black T-shirt and jeans that were no less flattering on him. The cross expression he'd worn when she'd last seen him had also been replaced; now he looked rueful, faintly penitent, even a little grateful that she had invited him in.

"I'm sorry," he said almost before she had the door fully closed behind him. "I was out of line."

"You were annoyed because I turned down your invitation to dance."

He shook his head. "No, it wasn't that. Not exactly. It was just…well, like I said, I'm sort of tired of tiptoeing around to keep from upsetting BiBi, especially for such a ridiculous reason. I mean, I've known her pretty much since we were both in diapers. It feels like I'm having to kiss up to one of my sisters or cousins, and I wouldn't want to do that, either."

"I can sort of understand that," she admitted. "I've never been one to mince words with my siblings, either. If Meagan had gone 'Bridezilla' on me during her wedding, I probably would have cut her down a size with a good talking to.

I just didn't want to make any waves with BiBi this weekend."

"I get that. And at first it didn't bother me. Like we said, the clandestine part was kind of fun. At first. But tonight…well, I would have enjoyed dancing with you. I didn't care who knew that I liked you and enjoyed being with you. And to be honest, I'm not so sure Corinna cares anymore, either. I think she has taken a closer look at me and decided I'm not really worth all the effort, and she's probably right. I think this big drama is all in BiBi's head…or maybe yours," he added candidly.

"Trust me, it's not all in mine," she muttered. Maybe BiBi had apologized for bringing up Steve Gleason's name, but that didn't mean she'd forgotten about him.

"Still…"

"I know. You wouldn't like feeling like you were sneaking around. That's not in your makeup."

Jason seemed taken aback by the insight. "Umm, maybe. Is it in yours?"

She shrugged. "I keep my private life private for the most part, but I don't normally feel the need for strict secrecy."

"You really think BiBi would be angry with you if she knew you'd been spending time with me, even though there's nothing between Corinna and me?"

He simply didn't understand, and she didn't know how to explain it. "Maybe she'd get over it, but I just don't want to deal with it right now. Especially since it will all be over tomorrow, anyway."

Something flashed across his face, an expression she couldn't quite read. He shut it down quickly, his features settling into an inscrutable half smile that didn't lighten his dark eyes. "Then I won't argue with you any longer. I came to your room tonight because I didn't want our short time together to end on a bad note."

"Neither do I. I'm sorry everything became so awkward."

He shrugged. "It wasn't your fault that things were so complicated between BiBi and Corinna and me this weekend. It will all blow over. Our families have been connected too long for this to get in the way for long. I'm just sorry you ended up in the middle of it. And I'm sorry we never got that last dance because of it," he added, reaching out to touch her cheek.

"Who says it's too late?" On an impulse, she stepped toward him, snuggling against his chest. His arms went around her automatically. Linking her hands behind his neck, she smiled up at him and began to sway. Very softly, she began to sing the chorus of "Bewitched, Bothered and Bewildered"—what she now thought of as their song.

His mouth curving into a more natural smile, Jason played along, matching his steps to hers, his hands sliding to her hips to hold her closer to him. She was very aware that she wore nothing but bits of satin and lace, and that his hands were very close to the lower hem of her chemise, which had risen when she'd looped her arms around his neck. The sexy glint was back in his eyes, reminding her of the night they'd met. All he lacked was the low-brimmed fedora.

His gaze locked with hers, he lowered his head to cover her lips with his. The lyrics to the song promptly fled her mind, but he didn't seem to notice the lack of music. Cupping her bottom to draw her even closer to his hardening body, he continued to rock her gently as he nibbled at her mouth, drawing her lower lip between his teeth for a gentle nip that sent a shiver coursing through her. Giving up all pretense of dancing, she leaned into him. Thin satin shifted against her sensitized breasts when she brushed against his chest, making her ache in a way that was both delicious and needy.

The nightie shifted higher, and his hands were

beneath it, stroking, squeezing, exploring until she gasped and shifted against him, unable to stand still. Only then did he lift her against him and turn toward the bed. Madison was already tugging at his T-shirt when he lowered her to the mattress, even as he swept her chemise up and over her head.

And to think she'd been tired when she'd left the dance, convinced she would go straight to sleep. Now, as she lay on her side smiling at Jason, who faced her in the bed, she felt wide-awake, unwilling to waste one magical moment in sleep.

"I should probably go. You need to rest for the wedding." Disinclination underlay Jason's noble offer, and he made no move to leave the bed, though she knew he would if she gave the word.

Instead, she shook her head against the pillow. "Stay just a little longer."

He reached out to trace her lower lip with one fingertip. "If it were up to me, I'd stay all night. But that's probably not wise."

"Probably not," she agreed reluctantly. "But just a few minutes more."

"I hope you're not too tired at the wedding tomorrow."

She shrugged. "A little makeup will do wonders. BiBi will never see any bags under my eyes."

His mouth twisted. "I'm sure she would blame me for that, too. Especially if she were to find out that I really could be blamed."

Madison made a production of shuddering. "Heaven help us both if that should happen."

He chuckled wryly. "Don't worry, I'm sure you'll look as stunning as ever tomorrow. And I'm going to be on my very best behavior. I swear I won't make one wrong step during the ceremony."

Remembering their tiff in the garden earlier,

Madison winced a little. "Your role really isn't that difficult," she conceded. "All you have to do is follow Allen's lead."

"I really wouldn't have missed the rehearsal if the call hadn't been important," he said quietly.

"I know. You said it was a longtime patient?"

"Not a patient, exactly, though I've seen her a time or two for minor infections. She's a family friend who needed me to interpret some news her family was given earlier today and to be straight with her about what it meant."

"I can tell by your voice that the news was bad."

"The worst," he agreed. "Her forty-two-year-old son has been diagnosed with stage four lung cancer. Already moved to the heart and the esophagus."

Madison felt her heart sink. "Oh. And they're just finding out?"

"Yeah. He didn't have health insurance. Put off going to the doctor despite the health issues he's been dealing with for the past year. He kept brushing it off as bronchitis, flu, smoker's cough…"

"And now it's too late."

"Yes. If they'd come to me sooner, I could have helped him work around the lack of insurance. But he lives in Marshall, and Linda said she didn't know he wasn't insured or that he was ignoring health issues until he collapsed at home. The doctors they consulted this week gave them all the facts, but Linda wanted me to give her some reason to hope."

"And did you?"

"I told her the truth. I told her there's always reason to hope, but that the odds against him are extremely high."

After a moment, Madison sighed. "That had to be a tough conversation."

"It was. I would have preferred to talk to her face-to-face at a better time, but she insisted on talking to me right then."

She remembered now how forced his smiles had been when he had rejoined the wedding party. How dark his eyes had been. She'd been so focused on BiBi's hurt feelings that she hadn't paid enough attention to those signs from Jason. "Why did she think you could tell her something different than the doctors they had already consulted? You aren't even an oncologist."

He shrugged. "She's known me a long time. She's a good friend of my mom's, and Mom thought maybe I could explain things a little more clearly for her. I talked to Mom later, and she said she tried to convince Linda to wait until Monday to call me, but Linda was determined that it had to be today."

"And you couldn't turn her down."

"Would *you* have?"

He sounded genuinely curious, so Madison took a moment to consider the question. Would she have been able to tell a grief-stricken old friend that she couldn't talk about her dying son because she had to practice walking in and out of a church?

"No," she said with a firm shake of her head. "I wouldn't have turned her down, either. And neither would BiBi. She would understand if she knew the circumstances."

"We'll just let it go. Like I said, she'll get over it, especially when I prove to be an exemplary groomsman tomorrow."

She gave a little smile, as he'd obviously intended, but was still thoughtful as she studied his handsome, relaxed face. "Really, Jason— don't you ever get tired of being everyone's go-to guy? It seems like you're on call 24/7, not only for your patients, but for your family and friends, as well."

She could tell that his first instinct was to deny that implication, but as she had done a few moments earlier, he paused to consider the question before answering. "I like my life," he said simply. "There's not much about it I would change, even given the chance."

"So you never feel like drop kicking that cell phone out the nearest tenth-story window?"

He laughed. "Every day. Doesn't mean I'd do it, but I'm only human."

She suspected some people might have cause to argue that. Jason seemed so darned perfect sometimes. She would probably feel quite flawed in comparison—if she allowed herself to go down that path.

Knowing it was their last, neither of them wanted the night to end. They lingered in the bed, kissing and talking softly about nothing in particular, and then took a leisurely shower together in preparation for Jason's departure. The shower lasted a while longer than either had planned, concluding with Madison pressed against the tile wall, her legs around Jason's waist, her arms locked around his neck. Both staggered a bit when they finally left the bathroom, knees weakened and rubbery, but Madison considered the past few hours worth every bit of the exhaustion she was sure to feel later. She could sleep when she got back home—at least when she wasn't on duty or traveling from one interview to another—but she'd had only this one last night with Jason.

He procrastinated just inside the door, avoiding the moment when he'd have to turn the knob and slip out. "So I'll see you later?"

"Of course. And I promise I won't treat you like a stranger."

His smile was a little crooked. "I won't expect you to throw yourself in my arms, but maybe we can have a friendly conversation at the reception?"

"I see no reason why we couldn't. Not at this point."

Apparently, Jason had gotten through to her in some respects. She was beginning to wonder, herself, why she'd been so paranoid about BiBi, so worried about possibly upsetting her friend. Madison and Jason were both free and single, and they didn't owe anyone explanations or apologies for spending time together. It had been unfair of her to treat him so coolly in front of the others. While she still preferred not to contribute to wedding gossip, she thought she and Jason could be on friendly terms without revealing too much of their history, brief as it was.

"I'll look forward to it. You're leaving right after the reception?"

"Yes. My flight leaves at nine tonight."

"Do you need a ride to the airport?"

"No, that's all arranged, thanks."

"I wouldn't have minded driving you."

"I know. But I'm not really big on goodbyes," she admitted, already feeling a little lump in her throat at the thought. "We'll just smile and shake hands when we leave the reception, the way we will with everyone else."

"I can handle the handshake, but I'm not so sure about the smile."

She moistened her lips and tucked a strand of hair behind her ear. "It has been…"

"Don't say it's been fun," he cut in quickly, holding up a hand. "That's too clichéd for our time together."

"Okay, I won't say it." But it had been fun, she thought wistfully. And so much more.

He looped a hand behind her head and tugged her toward him for a long kiss. "I'd like to hear from you sometime," he said when he released her and stepped away. "Maybe you could drop me an email to let me know where you'll be doing your fellowship next year? I'm curious about where you'll end up."

He told her his email address, a simple, easy-to-remember one she didn't need to write down. She wouldn't forget it. Because it was easier, she gave him one of her cards—the one with both her personal and her professional contact information. He'd have her phone number, but she doubted that he would use it. Even as they swapped the numbers and addresses, she suspected they wouldn't stay in contact for long, if at all. Once both got back into their hectic routines, it was likely that they would be too busy to keep up a long-distance correspondence, even with the ease of email. She envisioned a few quick notes spread further and further apart, until they stopped altogether, leaving them to remember this weekend with faint smiles and, on her part at least, wistful tugs of what-might-have-beens had they met under different circumstances and at a different time in their lives.

"Good night, Jason."

He kissed her one last time, then made himself turn and open the door. After checking the hallway, he slipped out, pausing only long enough to say, "Sweet dreams, Madison."

Only then did it occur to her that they hadn't used their playful nicknames all evening. It

was as if at some point during their hours together, they'd stopped thinking of each other as
intriguing strangers.

It was ridiculous for her eyes to burn with what
felt suspiciously like unshed tears as she walked
back to the tousled bed. After all, she would be
seeing Jason again in just a few hours. Sure,
they'd be saying goodbye for the final time not
long after that, but she'd been prepared for that
from the beginning. She'd never expected more.
Never even wanted more, she reminded herself
as she crawled beneath the covers.

But she thought she would miss him, anyway.

With the exception of the bride and maid of
honor, who were closeted in the dressing room
with their mother, the entire wedding party
gathered in the downstairs church fellowship
hall prior to the wedding. Phyllis, the wedding
planner, looked them all over with eagle eyes,

nodding in approval when she determined that everyone was there on time and fully dressed.

"You all look very nice," she pronounced, then glanced at her watch. "You have five minutes before the men need to move into the anteroom and the ladies to the foyer in preparation for entering the church. The ushers are seating the last of the guests now. Anyone who straggles in late will have to wait until the bride has entered before they can be seated."

"I'd hate to be a late arrival," Jason murmured into Madison's ear. "Even guests are likely to get a death glare from Phyllis if they don't follow protocol."

She smothered a giggle, knowing she would be the recipient of one of those death glares if she interrupted the planner's last-minute instructions.

Phyllis dismissed them and turned to bustle away. Checking her reflection in a gilded mirror on the wall, Madison touched up her lip gloss with the tube she'd carried with her to this last-minute gathering, then realized she'd left her bag locked in the upstairs dressing room. Her floaty, sleeveless purple dress—almost too pretty to be a bridesmaid dress, in her painful experience with former disasters—had no pockets. She could always tuck the small tube into her nosegay and hope it wouldn't fall out at an inconvenient time.

"Would you like me to hold that for you until after the wedding?" Jason offered, opening his jacket to reveal the hidden inside pocket.

"That would be great, thank you. I'll retrieve it at the reception."

"I'll trade it back to you in exchange for a dance," he said lightly.

She laughed softly. "It's a deal."

"Gentleman, ladies. Time to go upstairs."

Snapping to attention in response to the planner's command, the two groups separated. Madison glanced over her shoulder as she left the hall, smiling when she saw that Jason was also looking back at her.

BiBi needn't have worried about the ceremony. Thanks to the cooperation of everyone involved—not to mention Phyllis's iron-fisted organizing—it proceeded almost flawlessly. The bridesmaids gathered around BiBi in the church foyer for careful hugs and air kisses before lining up to file into the church, leaving the beautiful bride to enter on the arm of her proud, if slightly harried, father.

Everyone had agreed that BiBi's mood was better today. She was still high-strung and apt to overreact to the slightest problem, but that wasn't much different than usual for BiBi, especially with the addition of wedding nerves.

The church was gratifyingly packed with family and friends that the ushers had seated efficiently. Carl and his groomsmen were already arranged at the front of the church when Madison was given the cue to begin her walk.

Holding her nosegay of purple and white roses and baby's breath at her waist, she concentrated on her posture and pacing, as Phyllis had ordered, but she couldn't help noticing how nice Jason looked in his wedding finery. It was all she could do to keep her eyes on the bride and groom during the ceremony.

Both BiBi and Carl were glowing when they turned to face their guests as husband and wife. This formality had been a long time coming and they both looked deliriously happy, utterly satisfied with the choices they had made. Madison felt a bit misty as she watched them exit the church. It felt almost like the end of an era. Her long-distance friendship with BiBi wouldn't change greatly because BiBi was married now, but it was still different than when they had been single college girls having fun and blissfully unconcerned about the future.

Speaking of endings…

As soon as Allen and Lucy had started their

walk, Jason stepped forward to offer his arm to Madison. She wondered if he felt the slight tremor that coursed through her fingers when she lightly gripped his arm. She wasn't even sure herself what had precipitated it; just touching him seemed to have the power to make her knees weak and her hands unsteady. She kept her gaze fixed firmly on the exit door as they matched their steps. There was just something a little too unsettling about walking down the aisle with the man with whom she'd just spent a sizzlingly passionate night.

Back in a ballroom at the hotel, the reception was well underway an hour after the end of the ceremony. Because she'd chosen to have the wedding on Sunday afternoon and wanted to give the out-of-town guests time to travel home afterward, if they chose, BiBi had decided not to serve a wedding dinner. Instead, tables bulged with canapés, hors d'oeuvres, sweets—enough food to count as a light buffet suited to late afternoon. Madison saw several guests carrying full plates to the tables arranged invitingly around the room.

After a seemingly endless receiving line, toasts were made and the spectacular wedding cake was cut. Guests chatted, laughed, ate and drank. The bride and groom would have their first dance soon, opening the dance floor for the other guests. Everyone seemed to be having a great time, which Madison was sure would make BiBi happy.

As for herself, she was all too aware of passing time. She kept one eye on her watch while doing her part of the mixing and mingling. Every time she spotted Jason in the crowded room, he seemed to be surrounded by other people. So many of them bore a strong resemblance to him that she figured the D'Alessandro clan was well represented. Three women who had to be his mother and sisters hovered in his vicinity all afternoon. Like Jason, the sisters shared their father's dark coloring, while their mother was blue eyed and fair skinned, her gray-frosted, light brown hair swept up from a face that was aging beautifully.

She was sure he would introduce her to his family if she approached them, but something held her back. Maybe she preferred to remember him the way she'd spent most of the time with him, just the two of them, alone in the garden or in her room.

Suddenly the thought of shaking his hand in farewell was more than she could handle. She hadn't been kidding when she'd told him she wasn't a fan of goodbyes. On a sudden decision, she crossed the room to where BiBi stood chatting with some people Madison didn't know. Giving them a politely apologetic smile, she drew BiBi aside. "I'm heading out. The wedding was beautiful, Beebs. And so are you."

"You're leaving already?" BiBi shook her head in automatic protest. "Can't you stay a little longer? The dancing hasn't even started.

We haven't had a chance to talk since the ceremony."

"You still have a few dozen people waiting to speak with you," Madison pointed out, glancing around the crowded room. "You and I will have a long phone call when you get back from your honeymoon."

"Okay." BiBi gave her a fierce hug. "Thank you so much for everything. I'm so glad you were able to clear your schedule. I can't imagine not having had you here for my wedding."

"I wouldn't have missed it for the world."

"I love you, Maddie."

"Love you, too, BiBi. Be happy, okay?"

"I will. I am." BiBi took a step back, blinking hastily against the tears that threatened to streak her carefully applied makeup. "I'd call Corinna over to say goodbye, but she and Brandon disappeared a few minutes ago. I suspect they're plotting something crazy and tacky for when Carl and I get ready to leave."

"Still worried that she's using Brandon as a rebound from you-know-who?"

BiBi shrugged wryly. "She's having fun for now. I guess that's all that matters."

"Good for you for accepting that. Go back to your guests, BiBi. And have a wonderful honeymoon. Call me when you get home."

"I will. To all of the above."

After squeezing BiBi's hand, Madison turned toward the exit. She glanced back over her shoulder one last time before leaving. Half turned away from her, Jason stood among his family, one hand on Justin's shoulder as they all laughed at something one of them had said.

She had her own family waiting for her at home, she reminded herself as she walked out. A family she loved dearly, a job she found very fulfilling, several exciting and challenging decisions close ahead. It was time to put the weekend fantasy behind her and get back to her busy reality.

Chapter Nine

Jason sat in the spare bedroom he used as a home office, his computer in front of him, his phone close at hand. It was almost 10:00 p.m. on this first Tuesday in November and he'd just finished dictating all his patient notes. He still had several emails to answer and a journal paper he wanted to read. Yet he found himself leaning back in his chair, his pensive gaze fixed on the slim tube of lip gloss in his hand.

Just over two weeks had passed since Madison had slipped out of the wedding reception without a farewell to him. Though he thought he knew why she'd done so, it had still hurt more than he might have expected. At first, he'd written off his feelings as disappointment that there hadn't been another chance to chat with her, or at least to tell her goodbye. As the days had passed, he'd realized there was a lot more to it.

He missed her. Missed her smile, her musical laughter. The excitement and unpredictability she'd brought to his life. The passion that had flared between them whenever they'd been near each other. The fun.

He'd known all along that it was only a weekend romance, he reminded himself, as he had many times in the past two weeks. He'd never expected more. But he could admit to himself now that he had wanted more.

Had Madison lived nearby, he'd have made every effort to convince her to see him again. There could have been something between them, had circumstances been different. If she had lived closer. If she hadn't been so concerned about what BiBi would think.

Maybe, as a physician herself, and one with a close family of her own, she could even have understood his many obligations. An only child from a very small, not particularly close extended family, his ex-girlfriend Samantha had never quite comprehended the tight bond between the members of the Walker and D'Alessandro clans. Nor had she understood why he couldn't just put his work or his patients out of his mind when he left his office at night. He thought she'd tried— though he cynically wondered if that was mostly because she rather fancied herself as a doctor's wife. Unfortunately, she'd been unaware of all that entailed.

As for himself, well, he'd been fond of Samantha, but his feelings hadn't been strong enough to make him try very hard to hold on to her when he'd felt her drifting away. After a few weeks, he'd barely even thought about her. He wasn't proud of that fact, but it was only further proof that he and Samantha had been mismatched.

And yet, he had hardly stopped thinking about Madison in the past couple of weeks, even when he'd been bustling from one appointment to the next, fielding phone calls and text messages at the same time. Still staring at the lip gloss, he pictured her moist, shiny pink mouth, remembered the taste and feel of her, and he felt his body react dramatically and rather painfully to the memories.

He wondered how her fellowship interviews were going. Had she made a decision yet about her first-choice program? She would have to decide soon; the deadline was probably early to mid-December. Was Dallas still on her list of possibilities? Would hearing from him positively influence her decision—or send her running somewhere else to avoid any potential complications with him?

On a sudden impulse, he straightened in his

chair and reached for his computer. One thing he had learned during those too-few days with Madison was that it sometimes paid off to take risks.

Madison was taking a short caffeine break in a hospital coffee shop late Wednesday morning while she skimmed through her email on her phone. She took a too-hasty swallow of her coffee, almost burning her mouth when she saw Jason's email address on one of the unread messages. The subject heading read, Forget something?

Was he just getting around to chiding her for leaving without saying goodbye? She'd figured he wouldn't like that, but she'd hoped he would understand that she hadn't wanted their weekend to end with an awkward, public handshake. She opened the email.

Hi, sweet Esmeralda. You forgot your lip gloss. Since it's not my color, I'd be happy to send it to you if you like. I hope all is well with you.

It was signed simply, Jones.

Her throat suddenly tight, she set her coffee cup on the table and read the message again. She'd forgotten all about the gloss. She hadn't forgotten about Jason, not for one moment since she'd walked away from him.

His use of their silly nicknames told her he wasn't angry with her for the hasty departure. She was glad. She wanted him to remember her with a smile, not a frown. She certainly smiled whenever she thought of him, though she was all too aware that many of the smiles were a little misty.

No need to go to that trouble, Dr. Jones, she typed back quickly, but thanks for offering. Busy here, but I'm well. You?

She studied the breezy note for a moment before hitting Send. Did it strike the right tone? Friendly, not expecting a reply, but still open to one?

Her pager beeped and she sent the note before she could change her mind. It was only polite to reply, she reminded herself.

She found another message from him when she checked the next night before going to bed. Just as casually as before, he shared with her a humorous anecdote about his day that made her laugh. She was still smiling when she closed her eyes, deciding to wait until the next day to respond to give herself time to think of something equally amusing to say.

She sent him a funny story about her interview experience in Oregon. He responded with a laugh-out-loud recounting of something his young nephews had done. Within a few days, the daily emails had evolved from short and breezy to longer and chattier. They shared more tidbits from their days—some funny, some rather naughty, others more serious.

Madison told him about the fellowship programs she had visited and which ones appealed to her most and why. She mentioned casually that the program in Dallas still impressed her, and he responded with a light jest about how he couldn't imagine why she'd be interested in anywhere else. He said nothing more to influence her decision, and she had no idea how he really felt about her possibly moving closer to him.

Those daily messages were becoming a bit too addictive. While she still expected them to taper off, perhaps when they ran out of things to write, they showed no signs of slowing down a full month after she'd left Dallas. Several times each day she thought of things she wanted to share with Jason, and judging by the increasingly long notes from him, he was having no trouble thinking of things to say, either.

"Are you expecting a call, Madison?" her

mother, LaDonna Baker, asked after a Sunday lunch with the family.

Somewhat guiltily returning her phone to her pocket, Madison shook her head apologetically. "Sorry, Mom. Just doing a quick email check. Let me help you clear the table."

There was no lack of help with that task. Though Thanksgiving was less than two weeks away, the whole family had gathered for this lunch, as they did whenever they had an opportunity to all be together. She knew her siblings were both wearing their pagers, just as hers was in her purse, but none of them expected to be called to the hospital that day, to their mother's delight.

Fifteen-year-old Alice Llewellyn, Meagan's stepdaughter, chattered nonstop, as always, while the table was emptied and the dishes stowed away. There was always a lot of energy in the room when Alice was around. They all adored the teen and accepted her as a true member of the family, just as they did her attorney father, Seth. They were equally happy with Mitch's choice of bride, Jacqui, whom they had met when she accepted a position as Seth's housekeeper and nanny, back when he was still a single father and Meagan's neighbor. Someone else helped out in that household now that Jacqui was married to Mitch and had a house of her own to manage, but Jacqui still remained very close to Alice.

Each new member had integrated seamlessly into the family. Despite her occasional exasperation with her bossy older siblings, and her vague longings to spread her wings and try something new in her own life, Madison loved everyone here dearly.

She had noticed that Alice seemed a bit more hyper than usual that evening, and that Meagan and Seth kept giving each other smiles and meaningful looks. So it was no surprise when Alice finally burst out, "Can't we tell them yet? I can't wait!"

They had all just resettled at the table to linger over coffee or soda and a plate of homemade cookies. Jacqui, Mitch, Madison and her mom all looked from Alice's excitement-flushed face to Meagan and Seth, who were smiling ruefully. Somehow Madison knew what she was about to hear even before Meagan spoke.

"We're going to have a baby."

General pandemonium erupted around the table. Their mom, of course, was tearfully thrilled that she would soon have a grandbaby to spoil in addition to Alice. Everyone, including Madison, had to leap up and round the table for hugs and kisses and happy congratulations.

"I'm so happy for you both," Madison said to them.

Meagan looked a bit dazed, and Madison understood why. Her older sister had lost an ovary in an emergency operation three years earlier at the age of thirty-two. She met Seth while she was still recuperating from that surgery, and her life had changed so drastically since. Before, her career had consumed her, to the point that she had ignored her own health. Now there was balance. She was still a dedicated, hardworking surgeon, but she took time now for her husband and cherished stepdaughter and their goofy dog, for outings and vacations and the other things that added a little spice to life.

And now there would be a baby. Her sister's life would definitely get crazier and more demanding, but with the support of her husband, his daughter and her extended family, Madison had no doubt that Meagan could handle it all.

She saw a look pass between Jacqui and Mitch and she wondered how long it would be before they, too, made a similar announcement. She knew they wanted kids and planned to start their family soon. The family was changing, growing. Baby sister wouldn't be the center of everyone's concern anymore, not that she had been really for the past couple of years. Which was as it should be—even if she had been a bit spoiled by the attention, she thought with a self-mocking smile.

"So, have you made any further progress on deciding where to do your fellowship?" Mitch asked her a short while later, while everyone else was still talking babies.

"Still thinking about it," she admitted. "Every program I visited had pros and cons, of course, but they were all excellent in their own ways. I think I did well enough in my interviews and with my CV that I'll get my first-choice match— if I could decide which one that should be."

"Are you being drawn toward one in particular?"

Actually, one program was drawing her—but because she didn't quite trust her reasons for leaning that way, she was going to give it a lot more thought before she made a choice. "I'm still thinking about it," she repeated.

"Is it still a possibility that you'll choose to stay in Little Rock?"

"It's a possibility."

Her brother studied her face. "But not likely, is it?"

She shrugged. She was aware that Mitch had considered moving away several times—for medical school, for his residency, even more recently. Each time he'd come close to leaving, something had happened to hold him here, usually a family medical crisis. Now he and Jacqui had bought a house together here in Little Rock, where they planned to raise their family. She doubted that he regretted now the choices he'd made, but she had to follow her own path.

He touched his knuckles to her chin. "You know we all want the best for you, Maddie. But we all hope you don't go too far."

She leaned in to hug him. "No matter how far I go, you know I'll always come back. This is home, Mitch. That won't ever change, no matter what else does."

He kissed her forehead, then pulled back to search her face again. "Is there something going on with you, Maddie? Other than the fellowship search, I mean? You've seemed distracted lately—since you got back from BiBi's wedding, actually."

She forced a smile and shook her head. "Just busy. Maybe a little stressed about all the changes ahead. But excited, too."

"If you need to talk, you know how to reach me."

"And I know you're always there for me," she assured him affectionately. "Thanks, Mitch, but I'm really okay right now."

He didn't seem entirely convinced, but he let her get away with the evasion.

The week before Thanksgiving, Jason sat again in front of his computer, gazing rather glumly at the monitor. As much as he enjoyed the daily emails from Madison, they were becoming more frustrating than satisfying now. He didn't want to read just words from her, amusing as they were. He wanted to see her face when she laughed at his jokes or her own. Wanted to spend more time with her to see if he still found her as fascinating as he had during the scant four days they'd had together.

Twirling her tube of gloss between his fingers, he thought about his maternal aunt and her husband who lived in Little Rock. Though it hadn't been all that long since they had visited Texas, it had been a few years since he'd been to Arkansas. Maybe it was time for him to remedy that. He knew their door was always open to him… but would Madison close her door in his face if he showed up out of the blue after they'd already said their goodbyes?

Stumbling into her apartment Tuesday evening, Madison shrugged out of her jacket and threw it over the back of a chair. It had turned colder that week. Combined with the earlier darkness, it was clear that winter wasn't far away. Winters in Arkansas were generally fairly mild; they saw snow only a couple of times most years, and then only an inch or two. If she chose the fellowship in Massachusetts, she would see plenty of snow. Same with Oregon.

Dallas, on the other hand, had a climate very similar to Little Rock.

She pushed her hands through her hair with a weary sigh. She'd had a long day. Three admissions, one difficult chemical restraint, a bipolar patient who'd been doing so well for the past few days but had taken a dramatic turn for the worse last night. She loved her job, but there were days when she wondered if she should have learned to serve pancakes instead.

She hadn't had a chance to eat since lunch, which had been a long time ago. She was hungry, but first she wanted to wash her face and then check her email, something else she hadn't had time to do that afternoon. She hadn't heard from Jason in the past couple of days. She was sure he'd been busy, too, but he'd been taking time out of his hectic schedule to send her notes. Had it become too much trouble? She'd expected the correspondence to trail off eventually, but certainly not so abruptly.

She told herself she was making too much of this. She didn't really expect him to write every day. Didn't mean she would never hear from him again, just that he had other things to do. Other demands on his time. Maybe he was just running out of things to say to a woman he really didn't even know very well, despite everything they'd shared during that long weekend.

Even though she'd told herself not to expect anything, she was unreasonably disappointed when there was no note from Jason among the notices, requests and digests cluttering her inbox. A patient had told her a joke that morning she thought Jason would appreciate, but she was hesitant to send it to him. It was his turn to reply—and maybe it was silly of her to care about that little subtlety, but for some reason, she did. Maybe she'd drop him another note in a day or two if she hadn't heard from him, just to make sure everything was okay, and then she'd let it go. It wasn't as if she had that much extra time, anyway.

She was on her way to the kitchen, hoping to find something in her fridge for a quick dinner, when her cell phone buzzed. Figuring it would be one of her family, she lifted it to her ear without checking the screen, already frowning at the near-empty shelves in her refrigerator. She really was going to have to find time to make a grocery run soon.

"Hello?"

"Hi, Madison."

She almost tumbled face-first into the fridge. She shut the door quickly. "Hello, Jason."

"I hope I'm not calling at a bad time."

"No, of course not." She moved to the table and dropped into a chair, suddenly feeling a bit weak in the knees. A ridiculous overreaction to hearing his deep voice again, but there it was.

"I've enjoyed our emails, but I missed hearing your voice."

She moistened her lips. "It's good to hear from you."

She heard him draw a deep breath, as if he were working up courage for what he was about to say. Her fingers tightened on the phone in preparation.

"Listen, Madison—I'm in Little Rock, visiting my aunt and uncle for the holiday. So maybe— well, I thought maybe you and I could see each other while I'm here. If you want to, of course. And if you have time. If not, I'll understand."

He was here. In her town. And he wanted to see her.

She swallowed hard, trying to get her whirling emotions under control so she could think clearly. She couldn't imagine why she was reacting so dramatically to this call. Maybe she was just more tired than she had realized. "When would you like to get together?"

"Now." The answer was immediate, and a bit husky. "But I can wait until it's a good time for you."

She made herself pause for a few moments, trying to be sure she was making the right choice, and for the right reasons. That she was aware of all the possible complications and re-percussions of whichever decision she made. And then she nodded, as if he could see her through his phone. "Just one request."

He sounded resigned when he said, "I know. You want to keep it secret if we see each other."

She couldn't help but smile a little at his tone. "No, it's not that."

"Then what's the request?"

"Food. I'm starving and there's nothing in my fridge except mustard, outdated yogurt and one lonely egg."

A laugh was in his voice when he said, "I think I can do a little better than that."

She gave him her address.

"I'll be there in half an hour," he promised and disconnected without saying anything else.

Half an hour. After five and a half weeks, she would see him again in half an hour. She jumped to her feet, aware that she was scruffy and bedraggled from a long day at work. She wouldn't overdo it, but it wouldn't hurt to brush her hair and freshen up a little.

After fussing with her appearance, she made a quick dash through the apartment, straightening pillows, hiding bills and junk mail, rinsing a coffee cup and stashing it in the dishwasher. Should she make a pot of coffee? Was it too late? Maybe Jason would prefer a drink. Did she have anything on hand? Was the half bottle of white wine in her fridge still drinkable?

Jason's arrival sent the questions out of her head.

He stood outside her door, a half smile on his lips, a searching look in his eyes. "I hope Chinese is okay. I debated between that or pizza."

During the past weeks she had half convinced herself that Jason wasn't as attractive as she'd remembered, that she had idealized her memories of him. She saw now that the memories hadn't begun to do him justice.

"I love Chinese food," she assured him, standing aside to let him enter. Aromatic bags dangled from his hands. It appeared as though he'd brought enough food for a half dozen people.

"When I said I was starving, I didn't mean it quite that literally," she teased, motioning toward the dining table in her small, open apartment.

Dumping the bags, he chuckled. "I wasn't sure what you liked. Anything left over can be reheated for later."

"I should make some tea. Oolong goes well with Chinese. I'm pretty sure I have some in the—"

"I'd love some tea," he interrupted gently, moving toward her. "But first—"

She melted into his arms. As he'd said, the food could always be reheated later.

They got around to eating. Eventually. Sitting at her table wearing only his jeans and unbuttoned shirt, Jason scooped noodles with bamboo chopsticks and ate them while admiring Madison as she enjoyed her fried rice. Her hair was tumbled around her fresh-scrubbed face and she wore the short, black silk robe she'd worn in Dallas. She looked so beautiful it was hard to concentrate on the food.

"I wasn't sure if you would be glad to see me," he confessed.

She glanced meaningfully at their state of near undress. "I hope I managed to reassure you on that count."

Thinking back over the past hour, he smiled. "Yeah. Though I might need a reminder or two."

Her little giggle made him grin before he filled his mouth with another bite of noodles. He was relieved the food was good; he'd had to depend on directions and reviews found on his phone since he wasn't familiar with Little Rock take-out restaurants.

"Is your aunt expecting you back soon?"

He shook his head. "I told her I'm staying at a hotel. I haven't actually checked into one yet, but I didn't want to stay at her house where I wouldn't feel free to come and go as I wished."

"There's no need for you to find a hotel to-night," she said after only a momentary pause. "Though I'll have to get up early for work."

"That wouldn't bother me, as long as I wouldn't be in your way."

"No, not at all. Tomorrow's my last day of work for the week. After that, I'm off until Monday."

"The privilege of being a fourth-year resident."

"True. I scheduled these days off months ago, the same time I cleared those couple of days for

BiBi's wedding. I figured I would need the break after rushing around to interviews and the wedding and then more interviews, not to mention my responsibilities at work."

He nodded. "I put this week on my schedule some time ago, as well. I've got to be on call the whole week of Christmas this year, so figured I'd take this week, instead."

"You didn't mention you'd be visiting your family here for Thanksgiving."

He shifted a little uncomfortably in his seat, then figured he might as well be completely honest with her. "That's because I didn't decide to do so until a few days ago."

She studied his face, and it wasn't hard to tell what she was thinking. "You came to see me?"

Again, he chose candor rather than evasion. "Mostly. I mean, I'll visit my relatives while I'm here, but I was hoping to spend as much time with you as possible. I know it's short notice, and you probably have other plans for your days off.

I should have called and discussed it with you before just showing up on your doorstep, but like I said, it was sort of a spontaneous decision. I don't act on impulse very often, and I guess I haven't handled it very well…"

He was rambling. It was a almost a relief when Madison cut him off.

"It's okay. I'm glad to see you. And I don't have any big plans for the next few days. I was just going to kick back and relax a little before diving into all the preparations for the end of my residency program."

"I won't get in your way," he promised. "I can entertain myself. But if you have some free time…"

"I'll make time," she assured him, reaching out to cover his free hand with hers. "I'm glad you're here, Jason."

He laced his fingers with hers and allowed himself to relax. "So am I."

She seemed content with that explanation.

There was no discussion about what he hoped to accomplish with the visit; what, if anything, he expected beyond this latest long weekend adventure. And that was just as well, because darned if he'd know what to say. He still wasn't entirely sure himself why he'd been compelled to come to Little Rock, but he'd been honest when he'd said he was glad he had. He was more relaxed, more contented now, here in her rather scruffy little apartment, eating noodles at her table with its mismatched chairs, than he'd been since she'd left Dallas.

After the weekend ended, and he had to get back to his life there…well, it remained to be seen what would follow that. But he was becoming increasingly sure that he would still not be ready to say a permanent goodbye to Madison.

Madison was putting her coffee cup in the dishwasher, getting ready to leave for work the next morning, when Jason wandered into the kitchen, wearing nothing but a pair of jeans and a rather dazed look on his face.

"Where do you keep your adhesive bandages?" he asked, holding a wad of blood-soaked bathroom tissue to his forehead. "I didn't want to rummage around in your cabinets looking for any."

"What have you done? Sit down and let me look at that."

His hair still wet from his shower, he let her push him into a chair, though his expression was sheepish. "Shower accident," he explained succinctly.

She grimaced. "I forgot to warn you that the shower head is ridiculously low and the tub tiny."

"My own fault. I turned too abruptly to rinse off and caught the edge of the shower head with my forehead. It's not bad, just split the skin, but you know how a cut there will bleed."

To her relief, he wasn't downplaying the incident. It really was a shallow cut, certainly wouldn't need stitches or special care. A bandage would hold it together until it stopped bleeding, but he wouldn't even need that for long. "I just bought a new tin of bandages. I think I stashed them in the pantry—yeah, here they are."

Carrying the tin back to the table, she efficiently closed the still-seeping wound. "There you go. And a kiss to make it better," she added, leaning over to brush her lips an inch or so above the small bandage.

He grinned and pulled her onto his lap. "Do all your patients get that extra little treatment?"

Looping her arms around his neck, she shook her head. "I reserve that for a very select few."

"Glad to hear it." He covered her mouth with his.

She had to make herself get out of his lap a few minutes later, then laughingly ward off his hands as she headed for the door. She didn't want to leave…but she couldn't be late for work, either.

"Have a good day," he called after her. "I'll see you this evening."

Knowing that was true put a big smile on her face as he climbed into the car. Thinking of the inevitable goodbyes when he went back to his life in Dallas made the smile fade.

"So, tell me about this woman you're really in town to see."

Jason grimaced at the question from his aunt Lindsay Grant as he faced her across a table in a downtown Little Rock restaurant Wednesday. He would be sharing Thanksgiving with her, her husband and their daughter and son the next day, but he was treating his maternal aunt to lunch today while the others were all busy. He didn't bother with prevarications, since his family members had a knack for ferreting out the truth. Instead, he asked, "How did you know?"

"Justin," she said simply. "He connected the dots between a woman from Little Rock you met at a wedding last month and your sudden urge to visit your aunt for Thanksgiving. He mentioned it to your mother, who told me."

Jason groaned. He'd thought his mom was surprisingly accepting about his desire to spend Thanksgiving in Little Rock rather than at the huge, annual feast to be held at his parents' house in Dallas. Lindsay, Nick and their offspring often made the drive to Dallas to join that celebration, but had chosen not to do so this year because of other obligations this weekend, a tidy coincidence for Jason's last-minute plans. Now he suspected that his sweetly scheming mother had given her blessing because she was hoping a romance would ensue. She'd been prodding Jason to get out and date again ever since his breakup with Samantha last year. Apparently, she had approved of what she'd seen of Madison during the wedding. He just hoped neither his brother nor mother had mentioned the connection to anyone in the Lovato family, considering how skittish Madison had been about BiBi finding out about them.

Still slim and pretty in her fifties, his mother's youngest sister smiled at him, looking so much like his adored mother that he couldn't help returning the smile. "You don't have to tell me about her if you'd rather not, but I'd love to hear about her."

"There's not a lot to tell yet," he admitted. "I've only known her for a little over a month. We've spent only a few days together, though we've stayed in touch since the wedding."

She waved a hand dismissively. "Time doesn't matter. How do you feel about her?"

He chuckled wryly. "I'm nuts about her. But, you know, most people spend a little more time than our family generally does to get to know each other before making any serious commitments."

His mother's family were firm believers in love at first sight. Both she and each of her siblings had romantic stories of how they'd met and married their mates, and the success of all those marriages was a testament to their insistence that time was irrelevant when it came to matters of the heart. Several of his cousins had followed in the family tradition of marrying quickly, and so far, so good with the matches they had made.

As for himself...well, he'd dated Samantha for months before conceding defeat, but he admitted privately now that he'd known almost from the start that what they had would not last. Yet from the minute his eyes had met Madison's at that rowdy costume party, he'd known she was special.

It seemed he had more in common with his Walker kin than he sometimes realized.

"What's her name?"

"Madison Baker. She's a fourth-year psych resident. I asked her last night if she knew Nick, but she said she didn't." Lindsay's husband had practiced pediatrics in Little Rock for more than twenty years. "Her brother, Mitch, is a pediatric orthopedic surgeon at the children's hospital. Nick may know of him."

"He probably does. I don't know him, though."

"Her sister, Meagan, is also a surgeon, an attending physician at the med school. Jenny will probably get to know her when she starts med school next year." Lindsay and Nick's daughter planned to follow her dad into pediatrics, while younger brother Clay was more interested in mathematics.

"You're still assuming she'll be accepted. We haven't heard yet, you know."

Jason shrugged. "She'll get in. Having a dad in the local medical community is a definite plus, even if he isn't involved with the university. Not to mention her glowing résumé and stellar grade point average. She could have gone anywhere she wanted for medical school."

Lindsay had to concede. "Probably. But as selfish as it is, I'm glad she wanted to stay here.

She said she plans to practice in the state so she might as well train here and start building her professional network."

"Makes sense. That's part of why I stayed in Texas."

Lindsay gave him a look that held affectionate skepticism. "It had nothing at all to do with you wanting to stay close to your family?"

He shrugged a bit sheepishly. "Okay, maybe it did."

"I think it's lovely that you're so close to your family—both on the Walker and D'Alessandro sides. I'm sure you know how fortunate you are to have a whole lifetime of that sort of love and support."

"Of course I know."

No one knew better than a member of the Walker family how important those family ties could be. Having been separated as small children when they'd lost both their parents, his mother and her brothers and sisters had all been adults when they'd finally been reunited, thanks to his mother's decision to hire private investigator Tony D'Alessandro to locate her six missing siblings after her adoptive parents died. Tony had tracked down all five surviving siblings, and then had married his client, bringing Michelle into his own large, demonstrative, Italian-American family. The oldest of Michelle and Tony's four offspring, Jason had heard the story many times, but he never tired of it.

The youngest Walker sibling, Lindsay had been just a baby when she'd been adopted by a family in Little Rock, with whom she was still very close. Unlike their older brothers and sister, Michelle and Lindsay had no memories of those early years together, but they had formed very strong bonds with them all in the thirty-plus years that had passed since they'd reunited. Jason had always figured those years apart had reinforced a need and appreciation for home and family, especially for the older Walker siblings who had spent their childhoods in foster care.

That had to explain at least in part their tendency to swap lifelong vows as soon as they identified their soul mates.

"So, your Madison is a doctor from a family of doctors. She can certainly understand the demands on your time, just as you understand hers."

"She's not 'my' Madison, Aunt Lindsay. She's—"

Again, she waved off the distinction. "Maybe you could bring her to meet us while you're here? I'd love to get to know her."

"I don't know about that."

"Too early?"

"Too complicated."

She nodded her understanding. "Just know that I'm here for you if you need to talk."

He smiled. He was fond of all his aunts, both by blood and marriage, but he'd always had a soft spot for his mother's youngest sister. "Thanks, Aunt Lin."

"Or I could always talk to *her*," she added. "I

could tell her how foolish she would be not to grab hold of you and hold on while she has the chance. Perhaps she doesn't know yet what a great catch my nephew is."

Even though he knew she was teasing, he shook his head. "I think I'd better be the one to try to convince her of that."

She reached across the little table to pat his hand. "That shouldn't be so hard. Now, tell me all the gossip from home. Have Andrew and Aaron gotten into any scrapes lately?"

Chuckling at the dry question about his trouble-prone twenty-nine-year-old twin cousins, Jason launched into an anecdote about their latest misadventure, making his aunt laugh in delight. He was somewhat relieved that she had changed the subject, but thoughts of Madison weren't far from his mind as they chatted through the remainder of the lunch.

He had a long way to go before convincing Madison that he was a "great catch." First, he had to persuade her that they had a chance at having more than an occasional long weekend together.

Chapter Ten

Madison was in the habit of calling her mother every day after getting off duty, usually during her walk down the stairs and then to the parking lot. Those quick calls were just daily check-ins, with longer, chattier calls and visits on the weekends or the occasional evening, but Madison almost always remembered the long-standing tradition. When her phone rang as she headed toward the hospital stairwell Wednesday evening, she thought it might be her mom. Or—and her silly heart beat faster with the possibility—

perhaps Jason, confirming their plans for the evening.

Her steps faltered a bit when she saw BiBi's name on her telephone ID screen. She'd talked to BiBi only the week before. Was it only co-incidence that her friend was calling again the day after Jason had arrived in Little Rock…or was this call going to be extremely awkward?

Deciding she didn't want to try carrying on this conversation while walking down stairs, she veered toward the coffee shop.

"Hi, Beebs, what's up?" she said lightly. "Wait, hold on a sec—small latte," she requested from the barista, lowering the phone to her shoulder and pushing a bill across the counter with her free hand.

While waiting for her beverage, she spoke into the phone again. "Okay, I'm here."

"Bad time to call?"

"No, just getting off work." She nodded a thank-you to the barista and carried her latte to an empty table. "I can talk for a few minutes while I recharge with some caffeine. Is everything okay there?"

"Oh, yes, fine. Carl and I have a crazy day scheduled for tomorrow. Lunch with my family and dinner with his. We're going to be ridiculously full, but both families wanted us for Thanksgiving, so that was our compromise."

"Must be difficult juggling two families at the holidays." Neither of her siblings' spouses had families to juggle, so it hadn't been an issue during the Baker gatherings.

It was hard to imagine not being with her mother and brother and sister on Christmas or Thanksgiving or Easter, since she'd never missed a holiday with them thus far, but she supposed if she should ever marry someone with a close family of his own—say, in another state—compromises would have to be made. Not that she had any thoughts of marrying anyone for a while yet, she assured herself quickly. She still couldn't even make up her mind about where she wanted to do her fellowship!

"It's a nice problem to have, I suppose," BiBi answered contentedly. "We did this same crazy plan last Thanksgiving and it worked out fine, even though I swore I'd never want to eat again after that second huge meal."

Madison chuckled. She'd felt the same way after many a huge holiday meal at her mom's house.

"I heard Jason D'Alessandro is spending Thanksgiving with his family in Little Rock."

Madison's smile faded abruptly. So the timing of this call *hadn't* been a coincidence.

"Have you heard from him?" BiBi asked without waiting for a response.

"Yes, I have." Madison would not lie outright to her friend, whatever the repercussions. "I didn't know he was coming, but he called when he got to town."

She saw no need to add that he'd spent the

night with her. There was honesty—and then there was sharing too much.

"So there *was* a connection between the two of you at my wedding. I wasn't imagining it."

Madison chose her words carefully. "Jason and I met at the costume party, and yes, there was a connection. I didn't know until the next day that he was the man Corinna had a crush on—neither of you had mentioned a name to me. And he, well—"

"He felt free to get to know anyone he wanted, since he'd made it clear to Corinna that there was nothing between them and never would be," BiBi filled in somewhat bluntly.

"Yes. As soon as I realized who he was, I told him I thought we should keep our distance, because I didn't want to do anything to hurt Corinna or upset you. But, well, somehow we just kept drifting back together."

BiBi's sigh came clearly through the phone. "Now I feel guilty. You met a great guy and you couldn't have a good time with him because I was being such a diva. I still groan every time I remember how I acted to you, bringing up the past and all."

"I understood, BiBi." To a point. "You were protecting your little sister."

"Foolishly," BiBi admitted. "I mean, I wasn't doing her any favors to encourage her to think Jason might change his mind about her. I guess I just got carried away with all the wedding stuff, you know?"

"I know," Madison replied gently. "How's she doing?"

"She's great. She's been seeing Brandon quite a bit. I think there's some rebound involved, but she seems to really enjoy being with him for now, anyway. And he thinks the sun rises and sets with her, so that's what she needed right now. She told me she's a little embarrassed now about letting herself be carried away with her schoolgirl crush on Jason, especially since she's decided they'd never really work as a couple, anyway."

"That was awfully quick," Madison said somewhat doubtfully, wondering if Corinna was protesting too much.

"Well, really, she hasn't spent that much time with him in the past few years. She was away for college and then pharmacy school, and I think she romanticized him more than a bit—something that was encouraged by both families, for that matter. I think now she's seeing him a little more clearly. I mean, yeah, he's a great guy and all, but a woman would have to have the patience of a saint to put up with his divided attention!"

Madison wasn't quite sure what to say to that. Jason had made time in his crazy schedule to visit her that week, but that was no indication he could continue to do so in the future, even if they tried to maintain a relationship. And with the demands on her own time, she imagined people felt the same way about her—that a man would have to be very patient to accept the time she had left to offer. Of course, both of her siblings were in highly demanding medical careers, surgery being even more all-consuming than psychiatry, yet they'd both found mates who not only accepted those commitments but actively supported them.

"So, anyway," BiBi continued breezily, "if you want to see Jason, I'm okay with it. And I'm sure Corinna will be, too, once she has a little time to get used to the idea."

"Look, BiBi, it's not like Jason and I are a couple or anything. I mean, we've shared a few hours together, total. We'll be spending tomorrow with our separate families, then I assume he'll head back to Dallas soon."

"Still, something could happen. Especially if you choose the fellowship program here in Dallas. You know I would love it if you were that close, and I bet Jason wouldn't complain, either."

Even though BiBi couldn't see her, Madison resisted an impulse to roll her eyes. Talk about a complete turnaround! Now BiBi was going to push her into Jason's arms?

She knew newlyweds had a reputation for wanting to see all their single friends hooked up, but Madison would just as soon BiBi would back off this time. It had been more comfortable all around when no one else had known Madison and Jason were hanging out together. She'd never really expected it to become an issue, since she'd thought their goodbyes in Dallas had been permanent.

"Look, BiBi, I appreciate what you're doing. I didn't like feeling that I was keeping secrets from you, and I'm glad we can be honest with each other." To a point. "But you have to understand that as much as I like Jason, it's very unlikely anything permanent will develop between us. We're just having a little fun in our crazy schedules while we have some time off for the holiday. I'm sure before long we'll both be too busy to even send a text message."

She should have expected BiBi's loyal instincts to kick into high gear. "If that's true, then Jason's even more of an idiot than I thought. If he has any sense at all, he'll do whatever he has to do to keep you in his life."

There was no arguing with BiBi on this subject. Madison just hoped her friend would keep this conversation between the two of them. She was fairly confident in that respect. BiBi had her flaws, as Madison did herself, but gossip wasn't one of them.

Promising they would talk again soon, they wished each other happy Thanksgiving and then concluded the call. Madison drained her latte, then tossed the cup into the compostable bin before heading once again for the stairwell. She would call her mom from the parking lot after using the walk to her car to clear her head a little.

She still hadn't decided if she was going to mention Jason to her family tomorrow. Wasn't sure what she'd say if she did. How would she casually bring up a heated, impetuous and likely fleeting affair to her mother, sister and brother? It wasn't as if she hadn't had other rather brief, casual liaisons—but there was something different about Jason. About her convoluted feelings for him. And she wasn't sure she could discuss him without revealing too much to their all-too-discerning family.

She was afraid they might see that for the first time in her life, she had fallen hard and fast. As quickly as it had happened, as unlikely as it was to end happily, as bad as her timing— she was beginning to suspect she had tumbled precipitously into love with this ultra-responsible, deeply-rooted, commitment-overloaded family doc. And that scared her right down to her previously carefully guarded heart.

* * *

Madison had given Jason her spare key so he could let himself into her apartment if he got there before she did. He had asked her if she'd rather he check into a hotel for the remainder of his visit, and she had taken a moment to think before answering. While she couldn't help worrying a little that having him stay with her would become awkward—or that she would like it a bit too much!—she still found herself unable to ask him to leave.

His car was in the lot when she parked, and she felt her pulse rate accelerate at the thought of him waiting for her. She should have stopped for food, she realized as she climbed out of the car, shivering when a gust of cold wind tossed her hair and slithered into the open collar of her coat. She'd been too eager to see him again to even think about food until this moment. Considering the state of her pantry, they'd either have to eat leftover Chinese or order pizza unless he wanted to go out for a meal.

Letting herself into the apartment, she stopped in surprise when she was immediately greeted by delicious aromas. She could see Jason moving around in her little kitchen. He'd cooked for her?

There were flowers and candles on her table, she realized. And music drifting from the kitchen. She took a couple of steps, then paused abruptly when she recognized the song. An oldie. "Leather and Lace." She swallowed when Tom Petty wailed about never wanting to leave once he walked into his lover's house. Just the mention of the word *moonlight* in the song made her knees go weak as she remembered that first lovely kiss.

"Jason?"

His hum dying in his throat, he whirled, spoon in hand. "Oh. Hi. I didn't hear you come in."

His shirt was partially unbuttoned and the sleeves rolled up on his forearms. A lock of his dark hair fell over his forehead. He looked so sexy and charming pottering around in her kitchen that she couldn't help sliding a little farther into love with him.

She cleared her throat. "You cooked dinner?"

He chuckled. "I wish I could say yes. I'm just plating takeout. I thought you might be too tired to think about dinner. I hope you like barbecue."

She had to get a grip on her runaway emotions before she gave away too much to him. Tossing her coat and bag into a living-room chair, she spoke breezily as she moved toward him. "I'm from Arkansas. Of course I like barbecue."

"Hmm." Turning back to the bowls on the counter, he glanced at her over his shoulder. "If you want real barbecue, you've got to come to Texas, of course, but I'm told this place makes a passable substitute."

"Not getting into that argument." She headed toward the refrigerator. "But thanks for the food—even though you didn't have to provide for us again tonight. Wine or tea with your meal?"

"I saw your wine. I'll take tea."

She laughed. "You're in a mood tonight."

He caught her shoulder when she was within reach and spun her into his arms for a thorough kiss.

"A good mood," he said when he gave her a chance to breathe.

She released a long sigh, bracing herself against him for a moment until her knees remembered how to support her again. "Hmm, me, too. Now."

He smiled and picked up a platter to carry to the table when she started toward the fridge again. "How was your day? Other than long?"

"I've had worse." She would share a few tidbits with him during dinner. But first… "BiBi called me as I was leaving the hospital this evening."

Silverware clanked. Jason looked sharply at her. "Because of me?"

Filling two glasses with iced tea, she nodded. "Ostensibly to tell me happy Thanksgiving. But yes, really because of you. She heard through the impressive family grapevine that you were here in Little Rock, and she put two and two together."

"Was it bad?"

"Surprisingly…no." While they sat down to eat, she gave him a quick summary of the call—leaving out the part where BiBi had pretty much mapped out a future for Madison and Jason.

Jason shook his head in bemusement. "So we now have her approval to spend time together?"

"Something like that."

"Madison? Your friend BiBi? She's not quite normal."

Madison laughed. "Trust me, you aren't telling me anything new. But then, some people would say the same about me."

He made a show of considering, then nodded. "I can see that."

She laughed again, enjoying the banter. "Would you like some more iced tea?"

"Yes, please."

She stood and moved toward the fridge, sheepishly aware she wore a besotted smile as she did so.

"So, now that we have BiBi's blessing…"

Lying on the pillows snuggled next to Jason later that evening, Madison lifted an eyebrow in response to his out-of-the-blue comment. "You're still thinking about BiBi's phone call?"

"Thinking about it again," he corrected. "I was distracted earlier."

She walked her fingers up his bare, still slightly damp chest. "Pleasantly distracted, I hope?"

"Fishing for compliments?"

Grinning, she traced the faint indention in his chin with one fingertip. "No, but feel free to throw a few this way."

"You're beautiful. And sexy. And funny. And brilliant. And..."

Laughing, she covered his mouth with her hand. "Okay, that will do, thank you."

He kissed her fingers before tugging her hand away. "As I was saying about BiBi...does it make you feel better about us to know she doesn't mind?"

"I suppose. Though obviously I wasn't letting her disapproval stop me from seeing you."

"We just couldn't tell anyone."

"There was never any need to tell anyone," she corrected. "I said all along that I didn't consider us sneaking around. Just being discreet."

"So maybe we could be a little less discreet now?"

She looked at him in question. "I'm not sure what you mean."

"I'd just like to be able to come visit you without using my aunt as a cover story."

She lay very still, letting the impact of his

words sink in. "So after you go back this week-end…?"

"I'll still want to see you again. Did you really think I would just go back home and forget all about you? That didn't work before. I see no reason to think it will this time."

Her heart was suddenly beating so fast she could feel it in her throat. "Jason, I can't—"

This time it was he who covered her mouth with his fingers, understanding in his eyes. "I know what a busy time this is for you. I know you still have half your last year of residency to finish and I remember how hectic that period was for me. I know you haven't made your final decision about where you'll spend the next two years for your fellowship—though, I'm going to keep reminding you that Dallas is the most obvious choice," he added with a faint grin.

She knew her answering smile was weak at best. That decision of fellowship programs was becoming more complicated all the time.

She was beginning to worry about whether she would be able to decide independently of her feelings for Jason. If she chose Dallas, would it truly be on the merits of the program, or because she wanted to be closer to him, to have a chance for a future with him? If she didn't choose Dallas, would it be only because she found another program to be more attractive, or because she worried about the potential heartbreak and complications of living in the same town as Jason?

"All I'm saying is that I understand, and I won't make any great demands on your time," he went on, oblivious to her convoluted ponderings. "I'd just like to see you occasionally, when we both have a free weekend or holiday. It's only a little over a five-hour drive, or an hour flight. And in between, we have phones and computers."

"What you're describing is a long-distance romance."

He shrugged. "No need to label it."

"And the goal of this unlabeled liaison?"

Though he seemed amused by her wording, he answered enticingly, "Fun. Laughter. Escape."

Her pounding heart sank a little. Was that the way he still viewed her? His fantasy diversion from the crushing demands of his life at home? He had described an ambiguous future in which they went about their individual pursuits, getting together whenever it was convenient for both of them for a good time and some rousing sex. Friends with benefits. No real strings or commitments, no extra demands on their time, which was so limited already. She should probably be pleased that he was making it so simple.

And yet the description left her feeling somewhat hollow. Dissatisfied. Which was only further evidence that her feelings for Jason had already progressed far beyond attraction or even infatuation.

Telling herself she must be tired, or still rattled by BiBi's call or just generally not thinking clearly, she made herself smile and say lightly, "I always enjoy spending time with you, Jason. I certainly won't hang up on you if you call."

He chuckled, but she thought there was a certain discontent in his expression, too. Or was she merely projecting her own feelings?

She sighed lightly and nestled more deeply into her pillow. "I'm getting sleepy. Long day today. Another long day ahead tomorrow."

She was expected at her mother's at noon, bearing the dish she had to get up early to bake, and she would be expected to remain there until late afternoon, visiting and playing games and watching football on TV. Because her son would be having Thanksgiving lunch with his girlfriend's family, Jason's aunt Lindsay would be serving a later meal, a Thanksgiving dinner beginning at five.

Obviously, each of them could join the other's family for the holiday meal. Yet even after BiBi's call had removed some of the pressure for circumspection, and even though Madison was certain her family would welcome another diner at their Thanksgiving table, she'd still hesitated to suggest it. When she'd tentatively floated the possibility past Jason, she could tell he was just as uncomfortable with the idea.

Still, it seemed only polite to offer one more time. "You're sure you don't want to join my family for lunch tomorrow?"

He smiled and brushed a strand of hair from her cheek. "Thank you for asking, but I won't intrude on your family. Not this time, anyway."

He was definitely leaving the possibility open for future holidays together, she realized. Jason seemed serious about wanting to maintain a relationship with her after he returned to Dallas, as undefined and long-distance as that relationship might be. Filled with a new sense of budding optimism, she envisioned a vague future with Jason as an important part of it—and it made her happy, she realized with a little thrill of excitement and nerves.

As if making sure she wouldn't waste time fretting about him, Jason added, "I'll be fine hanging out here watching TV for a while, and Aunt Lindsay told me I was welcome to show up early at her house to hang out with my uncle. Have a great time with your family."

"You do the same."

"I will." He leaned over to kiss her. "Good night, Madison."

She snuggled into his shoulder, trying not to think about how empty her bed would be this time next week.

Perhaps it was a demonstration of her state of mind that Madison was acutely aware of the vibes between her siblings and their spouses during their holiday together. The shared looks and smiles. The unspoken thoughts that obviously passed between them when something struck them as funny or particularly interesting. It had never particularly bothered her to be single in a room full of couples because she had always been content with her own company, but still she found herself missing Jason that day. Several times she pictured her sharing a laughing glance with him or thought of how much he would enjoy a certain anecdote told by one of her family members. She thought he and Mitch and Seth would get along very well, and she had no doubt that the women would love him, as women always seemed to do.

How could she be so keenly aware of his absence today when he'd never even spent time with her family? When she'd spent so little time with him, herself, actually?

He had implied that there would come a time when they would meet each other's families. She would like that. From what she had seen of them at BiBi's reception, his family had looked nice. Maybe sometime during the Christmas holidays she could take a day or two to pop over to Dallas. She wondered if Jason had any plans for New Year's Eve....

"Hello? Maddie? Where are you today?"

Blinking rapidly in response to her brother's teasing question, Madison looked up from the game pieces she'd been staring at so blankly. "Umm, sorry. Is it my turn?"

"It is," Alice said from across the game table. "Are you okay?"

Smiling fondly at her niece, Madison nodded. "I'm fine, thanks, hon. Just have a lot on my mind."

Madison's mother and sister-in-law had chosen to sit out the games this time. Her mom sat in a chair looking through the newspaper ads for tomorrow's Black Friday sales while Jacqui sat nearby with her latest knitting project. Jacqui looked up from her intricate project to ask, "Don't you have to rank your program choices soon?"

"I've got about two weeks."

"I promised myself I wouldn't try to influence you, dear, but is there any chance you'll choose to stay here in Little Rock?"

Madison answered her mother's question gently. "Wherever I choose to go for my fellowship, you won't have to worry about us losing touch, Mom. I'll still call every day, when possible, and I'll be home for holidays and visits whenever I have the time off."

"You'll be leaving us, won't you?" Her mom seemed resigned to the inevitability.

"Probably for the fellowship," Madison conceded. "As good as our program is, I've spent the past eight years here. I think I should get some training elsewhere so I'll have a broader experience to build on in my future career."

"As much as I'll hate to see you leave, I'm sure you know what's best for you."

Madison wished that were true. At the moment, she wasn't feeling at all certain she knew which path to take for her future, either professionally or personally.

"Do you have a feeling about which program you'll rank first?" Mitch asked.

"I'm considering Dallas," she said casually, then added, "Or maybe Oregon."

"I vote for Dallas," Alice piped up. "It's closer. And we could come visit you and see a Cowboys game. Or the Rangers! And we could go to Six Flags and maybe ride horses and stuff."

Seth tugged at one of his daughter's brown curls. "No one said you get a vote, kiddo. Madison's not going to choose a program based on the sports teams you like best."

"I thought we were playing a game here," Madison said in an attempt to change the subject.

Alice sighed gustily. "It's your turn. We can't play until you do."

"Oh, right. Sorry." Hastily, Madison picked up the dice.

It wasn't long until the conversation drifted off Madison, to her relief, and onto the other exciting family development. Alice chattered about how eager she was to meet her new baby brother or sister. She assured everyone she would be thrilled to babysit anytime her services were needed, to the amused skepticism of her elders, who figured the novelty would wear off quickly enough when she had a date or a chance to attend a party with her high school friends.

"You're feeling okay, Meagan?" Madison asked, noting that her older sister certainly looked to be in glowing health.

Meagan nodded happily. "So far, so good. Not even any morning sickness."

"I never had morning sickness, and neither did my mother," their mom commented. "I guess it runs in the family."

"Instead, you had to pass down your ragweed allergies," Mitch complained humorously. "Thanks a lot, Mom."

After everyone chuckled at that, Meagan commented, "Maybe if I'd had some morning sickness, I'd have realized I was pregnant before two and a half months had passed. You'd think a doctor would be more tuned in to such things, but since my surgery, I haven't been all that regular and there was the chance I wouldn't be able to get pregnant at my age and with only one ovary."

"If you're going to start talking about women's issues, I'm out of here," Mitch complained wryly.

Alice rolled her eyes. "You're a doctor, too, Uncle Mitch. Geez."

He grinned. "I'm a bone surgeon. Basically a carpenter. I get to use power tools and everything—no gynecological issues involved."

"You should have been at that dude ranch when I was trying to remember how to deliver a baby," Madison said with a shake of her head. She'd told her family a little about the incident, saying only that she and another doctor who was equally inexperienced with labor and delivery had handled the birth. They'd been too amused by her humorous recounting to ask many questions about her involuntary assistant.

Madison thought of the conversation with her sister again when she climbed into her car a couple of hours later, carefully storing a stack of leftovers in disposable containers on the seat next to her. Something Meagan had said nipped uncomfortably at the back of her mind. Sitting behind the steering wheel before turning the key, she mentally replayed her sister's account of how long it had taken her to realize she was pregnant.

Swallowing hard, Madison counted weeks on her fingers. When she had to switch to her other hand, she felt the bottom fall out of her stomach.

She'd been so busy and so distracted for almost six weeks that she hadn't paid attention to her own cycles. It had never even crossed her mind that she could be pregnant. She and Jason had been so careful. They'd used protection every time—except that one last time in Dallas, in the shower, she remembered rather sickly.

One time. Was her luck really that bad?

Maybe it wasn't true. Like Meagan, she had a history of minor gynecological problems which had led to menstrual irregularity in the past. She was a few months overdue for her annual checkup. Maybe this was something else entirely. As she had just stressed to her family, she was not an ob-gyn.

Still, she thought she would make a stop on her way home. After that...well, she couldn't look that far ahead just yet.

Jason had no clue what had gone wrong. Was it something he had done or said? Had Madison's day with her family caused her change in attitude toward him? Had she reconsidered all he had said to her last night and decided he had no place in her future?

The problem was, she wasn't talking. For the first time since he'd met her—admittedly, not that long ago—her usually animated, expressive and approachable face was completely closed to him.

He'd returned to her apartment from his aunt's house at just before nine. Rather than letting himself in with the key, which seemed a bit presumptuous when she was there, he'd rung the bell. Her expression had been distant from the moment she'd opened the door to him. She'd responded to his conversational overtures politely, somewhat absently, little more than monosyllabically.

Something was definitely wrong.

She asked him courteously if he wanted anything to eat or drink. He replied with a laugh that he couldn't possibly fit another bite into a stomach already filled with his aunt Lindsay's cooking. She didn't laugh in return.

His phone beeped with a text message alert. Glancing at the screen, he saw that it was from one of his cousins, wishing him a happy Thanksgiving. He'd talked to all his immediate family members earlier, and he would answer this message later. No rush, he told himself, setting the phone aside. He had more important issues to concern him now, he thought as he studied Madison's somber face again.

"Is everything okay with your family?" he asked cautiously. It was none of his business, of course, if there had been a family quarrel or some other unpleasantness that had affected her mood, but if she needed to talk, he wanted her to know he was here for her.

"Yes, they're all fine, thank you. And yours?"

"Yeah, great. I enjoyed visiting them. It's rare we have a chance to chat in small groups like that. Usually on holidays there's such a huge mob of family it's hard to talk to anyone one on one."

"I'm glad you had a nice visit."

He couldn't take this any longer. He got the impression that her odd mood had nothing to do with her family and everything to do with him. "Okay, Madison, what's going on? Is there something you want to say to me?"

Still wearing that inscrutable mask, she tucked her hands inside her elbows. "I was just wondering—when were you planning to head back to Dallas?"

He felt his left eyebrow rise. "Kicking me out?"

It had been a joke, of sorts, but when she didn't smile, any faint amusement he'd felt faded abruptly. "You *are* kicking me out?"

"Of course not," she said, though she didn't sound entirely sincere. "It's just that I'm going to be pretty busy the next couple days, and I wouldn't want you to be bored. I had some plans for the long weekend, and I'd kind of hate to cancel them at this point because I'm going to be so busy in the coming weeks."

"I told you when I arrived without notice that I didn't want to get in your way if you had other plans for this weekend," he reminded her evenly.

"I meant it. All you have to do is tell me and I'm out."

She avoided his gaze by brushing at a nonexistent piece of lint on her dark pants. "Maybe it's best. It could become a little awkward."

"It?" he repeated, trying to understand.

"Us," she clarified, waving a hand in a vague gesture that included them both.

This just kept getting worse.

"Madison—are you breaking up with me?" He didn't know how else to phrase it.

She seemed to draw even more tightly into herself, if that were possible. Again, she spoke without actually looking at him. "I would hardly define it that way. Breaking up would imply we had something more than—well, than a weekend fling. Even though it was technically a few days more than a weekend."

The extent of the pain that shot through him in response to her use of the word *fling* let him know just how hard he'd fallen for Madison, no matter how brief their time together had been. Apparently, he'd inherited the full Walker capacity for tumbling into love almost overnight—but unlike his fortunate relatives, he had fallen for someone who clearly didn't return his feelings.

"So, it's over?" As much as he'd hated to ask, he needed the answer.

"I just think it's best for now," she muttered with a nod. "The timing just couldn't be worse."

That sounded like an excuse if he'd ever heard one. Hadn't he assured her earlier that he wouldn't interfere with her career plans? He would have been content, for the most part, to see her when it was convenient for them both, hoping those encounters, no matter how brief, would eventually lead to a future together. He hadn't promised it would be easy to maintain a relationship under those circumstances, and he had no doubt it would have been frustrating at times, but he thought they could have made it work, if Madison had been willing to give it a try. Apparently, she didn't think it was worth the effort.

"Then I won't interfere with your busy schedule any longer," he said, heartache erupting in cool temper. "I'll just get my bag and clear out of your way."

"Perhaps that would be best," she repeated.

The fact that she didn't even attempt to detain him just cut even more deeply. He stalked into the bedroom and grabbed his bag, still finding it hard to believe it was ending this way between them.

"Take care of yourself," he told her gruffly as he moved toward the door. "I wish you the best of luck in your future."

"Thank you. Good luck to you, too."

He didn't even know what to say to that. Looking over his shoulder one last time, as if to imprint her face in his memories, he let himself out, closing the door with a sharp snap behind him.

Chapter Eleven

Madison lasted all of three minutes after Jason left before bursting into tears.

She had handled that whole scene abysmally. For a psychiatrist, she had no skills at all when it came to dealing with her own emotional crises. Maybe she should have chosen another specialty, she thought with a miserable sniffle.

She paced the living room for an hour, alternately crying and cursing herself for being an idiot. Every time she almost got a grip on her tumultuous emotions, the thought of never seeing Jason again set the tears flowing again.

Her hands were shaking when she poured herself a glass of water and carried it into the living room. She sat on the couch, sipping the cold liquid without even tasting it, staring blankly at nothing while she tried to think rationally.

She had certainly gotten herself into a mess this time. Why did she always have to be the one in the family to do things so differently? Her siblings had very traditionally fallen in love and married before starting their families. Meagan and Mitch had always predicted that Madison's predilection for impulse would get her into trouble someday. Looked as though they were right.

Pregnant. She drew a shaky breath, still trying to come to terms with the word several hours after seeing the results of a home test. She knew she would have to have the results confirmed, that there was a chance it was a false positive… but deep in her heart, she knew it was true. What she didn't know was what she would do next.

She would have to talk to Jason eventually. It was only fair. And she knew exactly what his overdeveloped sense of responsibility would lead him to do. She couldn't bear the thought of him making some big, noble sacrifice for her sake.

He had viewed her as the opposite of all the people depending on him, making demands on him, expecting him to take care of them. She had a lot of decisions to make in the near future, but she was fully capable of making them and dealing with the consequences on her own. She could take care of herself—and this new life, for that matter, if that were her ultimate decision. It wouldn't be easy, but she could figure it out.

Maybe she didn't need Jason in her life, but she certainly had grown accustomed to having him there in a very short time, she thought sadly. Maybe they could have had a special relationship in time, but this development had changed everything. She would never know now what might have unfolded between them naturally.

The ringing of a phone made her start and almost spill her water. It wasn't her ring tone, she realized abruptly, searching the room for the source of the sound. She spotted Jason's phone on an end table just as it buzzed again.

Groaning, she stared at the device in indecision. She wouldn't feel right answering his phone, especially under the circumstances. But what if it was an emergency? She had no idea where he'd gone or how to reach him. How long would it take him to notice his phone was missing? Would he come back for it, or would he simply get a new one to avoid having to see her again?

She could hardly blame him if that was his decision. He'd looked angry when he'd left. He must think she'd lost her mind, the way she'd acted that evening. With no warning, she'd all but thrown him out of her apartment, and after they'd had such a lovely breakfast together that morning.

What was wringing her heart in painful spasms was the memory of his expression when he had looked at her just before he'd walked out. In addition to confusing him and angering him, she was pretty sure she had hurt him. And that had never been her intention.

His phone stopped ringing, and she assumed the caller had been transferred to voice mail. She would have to return his phone to him, of course. He'd mentioned his uncle's name, Dr. Nick Grant, a local pediatrician. Madison didn't know him, but she could find him. Tomorrow, maybe.

When she heard the tap on her door, she knew it wouldn't be necessary for her to track down his family. Jason had returned to reclaim his phone for himself.

Drawing a deep breath, she set the water glass on the coffee table, then dashed a hand over her cheeks before moving to the door. She only hoped she could bluff her way through the next few minutes without melting into a miserable puddle at his feet.

She had his phone in her hand when she opened the door. She tried to keep her face shadowed when she held it out to him, hoping to hide the ravages of her tears. "You forgot this."

"I know. I just realized it." He accepted the phone, then planted his hand on the door as if to keep her from closing it in his face. "Madison, could we talk for a minute? I really hate to end our time together on a bad note."

"I don't want to do that, either," she confessed. "It's just—well, it's late."

"I know. I won't stay long. I just—" His words trailed off as he searched her face, seeming to really see her for the first time since she had opened the door. She looked quickly away, but it was too late. "Madison—"

"You'd better go," she whispered. "I'll call you later, okay?"

But he was already inside, the door closed behind him, his hand on her chin as he gently lifted her face. "You've been crying."

"I'm fine." She wasn't, of course. She was a mess. And she wanted nothing more than to burrow into his arms and just lose herself there until she regained her usual equilibrium and self-sufficiency. But she wouldn't do that. She wouldn't be like everyone else in his life, depending on him to solve all their problems.

"Madison, talk to me. What's going on? Is it something with your family? Is there anything I can do to help?"

His obvious sincerity made tears hover again, but she blinked them back impatiently. She was not a crier! Her hormones must be in a real mess for her to behave this way now. "Thank you for your concern, but—"

Jason shook his head impatiently, though his tone was still gentle when he said, "It isn't just concern. I care for you, Madison. I think I fell in love with you the first night I met you. And seeing you hurting like this—well, it's tearing me apart."

* * *

Her mind spinning dizzyingly, Madison had to make an effort to keep her jaw from dropping. Jason was in love with her? He couldn't possibly be! There hadn't been enough time for that.

But hadn't she fallen in love with him in that same ridiculously short time?

His mouth twisted wryly as he studied her face. "I didn't mean to blurt it out that way. I understand why you look stunned. You don't know my family history. Haven't heard the stories about how many of my relatives fell in love at first sight, and then turned that first infatuation into a lifelong commitment. I never expected it to happen to me—but then I met you. And there it is."

"Jason—"

"Now I've really scared you off, haven't I?" He shook his head in self recrimination. "I can't seem to do anything right where you're concerned. I'm sorry, this is all new for me."

"It's new for me, too," she murmured. "You have no idea."

Something in her tone seemed to give him renewed hope. "Are you saying you have feelings for me, too?"

She sighed. She simply couldn't lie when asked a direct question.

"I'm crazy about you. But—" she added quickly, holding up a hand when he moved precipitately toward her "—there are still so many issues we have to discuss, Jason. Like I said, you have no idea."

He stopped, but there was a new glint of determination in his dark eyes that made her a little nervous. "I understand. Your career is important to you, as it should be, and this is an awkward time for you. I told you before, and I meant it, I won't get in your way. If you choose to train someplace other than Dallas because you think another program would be better for you, then I'll back you all the way. I can practice where you are—there's always a job for a primary care physician."

She blinked. Had he really just offered to walk away from his life in Dallas for her? "You would do that? Give up your practice to be closer to me?"

"I didn't say I would give up my practice," he reminded her with a faint smile. "I said I'd practice somewhere else. The job's important to me, the geography—not so much."

She sank onto the couch, her knees threatening to give out on her.

Jason took a seat next to her, still looking at her rather anxiously. "We don't have to make any hasty decisions. You've still got a couple of weeks to rank your programs, right? And then you won't know your match until March, and it'll be a couple months after that before you finish your residency.

"That will give me plenty of time to court you properly," he added with an endearing smile.

"To convince you we belong together. No pressure at all. But unless you send me away again for good, be prepared for me to wage an all-out campaign to win your heart."

He probably thought he was helping by reminding her of those dates she already knew so well. Maybe he believed she would take comfort from being assured that he wasn't rushing her, that there was plenty of time for their relationship to progress before any big changes had to be made. But then, Jason wasn't aware of all the facts. He couldn't know that the thought of those passing months, and the drastic developments they would bring, terrified her.

"You're offering so much," she whispered. "And it means the world to me that you're willing to do so, not that I would expect anything different from you, considering everything I've learned about you. But I refuse to add to the burdens already in your life. I won't be someone else expecting you to deal with my problems."

He looked confused. "I don't know why you keep saying that. If I've given you the impression that I'm unhappy with my life, or the responsibilities I've chosen to accept, then I need to dissuade you of that belief. I'm happy with the choices I've made. Maybe I complain sometimes—I'm only human, after all. And maybe I need an occasional escape from the pressure, as you, especially, would know. But overall, there's not much I would change. Except to keep you near me. If that means relocating, that's not such a big deal. I'd still remain close to my family and friends in Dallas, just as my family here in Little Rock and my cousins who've settled elsewhere have done."

He made it sound so easy, she thought with a catch in her throat. Of course, he didn't know everything yet. She reached rather desperately for her water glass, needing to soothe her tight throat.

"I know I have a reputation for being Mr. Responsibility," Jason said a bit sardonically before she had taken the first sip. "Both BiBi and my sisters have teased me with that enough times. And I'll admit, my obligations have scared off a few women in the past, which I'm sure they told you. The thing was, I was never willing to make any drastic changes for the other women I've dated. I mean, like the rest of my extended clans, I've always wanted a home and a family of my own, but I always intended to wait until I found the right person. I was waiting for you."

His mention of wanting a family made her hand jerk spasmodically. Water splashed across her lap. She groaned, wondering just how many more messes she was going to make that evening!

Jason jumped to his feet. "Hang on, I'll get a towel."

Setting her glass on a coaster, she swiped ineffectively at the wet spots on her slacks. "Thanks, I—oh, wait. Jason!"

But it was too late. He had already disappeared into the bathroom.

She was halfway off the couch when he reappeared moments later, a cardboard box in his hand, a stunned look on his face. "Madison?"

She swallowed hard.

"Is this— You're—?"

"I was a little slow figuring it out," she muttered. "It just occurred to me today that I— Well, anyway, it's always possible that it's a false positive, but I have a feeling it's true."

He looked from her to the box and then back again. "This is why you were so upset when I arrived earlier. This is why you sent me away, why you said you didn't want to be a burden to me."

She nodded miserably. "I think it happened that last time in Dallas," she muttered. "In the shower?"

Though he still looked almost as dazed as she'd been feeling for the past few hours, Jason gave her a taut little smile. "We both seem to be prone to shower accidents. Maybe we'd better stick with baths in the future."

She glanced at the almost-healed cut on his forehead, unable to even try to smile in return. "I know you didn't sign on for anything like this. I don't want you to feel like you have to be here for me. I can handle this. I'm not expecting anything from you, and I won't blame you in the least if you—"

"Madison." Tossing the box on the couch, he took several rapid steps toward her and caught her hands in his. "Did you not hear me earlier? I all but proposed to you before it even occurred to me that you could be pregnant. Heck, I *would* have proposed if I hadn't thought it would scare you away again. I'm that certain of my feelings for you. Do you really think this changes my mind?"

Propose? *Marriage?* Her mind whirled. "I, uh—I don't—"

"We still have time," he reminded her, squeezing her hands more tightly. "We don't have to make any big decisions right this moment. We have a lot of talking to do, and we'll get to it, now that all the cards are on the table. But first—"

He tugged her into his arms to hold her tightly as he kissed her. She clung to him, returning the kiss with a renewed surge of hope mingled with the doubts and uncertainties.

"I'm not going anywhere," he told her when he finally lifted his head. "Not unless you send me away again."

"I don't think I have the strength to send you away again," she confessed. "I told you once before—I really hate goodbyes."

"You won't have to say them again to me. Not for long, anyway. I can take a leave of absence from work for a few months to join you here while you finish your residency. It's not going to be easy for you in those last couple of months, but I've seen plenty of pregnant residents who were able to perform their jobs quite satisfactorily. I mean, if that's what you choose, of course," he added, as though suddenly aware that he was taking a great deal for granted.

She, too, had worked alongside expectant physicians. Even medical students. She knew it could be done. She had always vaguely envisioned herself having children someday, yet still continuing her career, just as her sister, Meagan, would do. She'd just never expected it to happen so soon.

But then, she had never done things exactly the same way as everyone else, she thought, finally finding just a glimmer of her usual sense of humor again.

"You almost smiled," Jason commented, touching her lips with one fingertip. "Does that mean you're starting to feel a little calmer?"

She nodded slowly. "I think so. I guess I sort of lost it there for a while."

"I don't blame you. I'm a little befuzzled, myself."

His choice of adjective made her laugh softly. "I'm sure you are."

"We can do this, Madison."

She drew a steadying breath. "Maybe we can, at that."

So many decisions remained to be made. So many discussions and compromises. But he had almost convinced her that what they had was worth fighting for.

"I love you," he said, giving her even more reason to believe.

"I love you, too." The words felt so strange and new on her lips, but somehow so right.

"Looks like we're about to embark on a new adventure, Esmeralda."

She wrapped her arms around his neck. "So, you think you're up to it, Jones?"

"Oh, I think I can definitely be up to it," he

quipped, hauling her closer, a laugh in his dark eyes now.

A new adventure, she thought, lifting her mouth to his. A new love. A new family. And it had all begun with a kiss in the moonlight.

All in all, she thought that had been a very promising beginning.

The wedding took place on New Year's Day. Jason and Madison had agreed that the first day of the new year was as good a time as any to begin their new adventure.

Wearing a cream-colored, tea-length dress that framed a modest amount of cleavage and floated softly over her tummy, which was just beginning to expand, Madison mingled happily with her guests after the simple ceremony. It hadn't been easy to keep the event small, considering the size of Jason's family, but they'd managed to convince his extended relatives that they wanted an intimate affair and would celebrate with a big party in a few months, after Madison completed her residency.

She still hadn't heard for certain where she'd been accepted for her fellowship, but she had ranked Dallas as her first choice and she felt reasonably confident she would get in. She was content with her choice, both because it was a very good program and because she and Jason would be comfortable there with his family nearby and her own within a few hours' drive.

They had exchanged their vows in the little church Madison had attended all her life, followed by a small reception hosted by Jacqui and Mitch in their lovely Craftsman-styled house in a historic Little Rock neighborhood. To the delight of everyone, Jacqui and Mitch had announced at Christmas that yet another member would be joining the family within the next few months.

Having adjusted to the surprise events in Madison's life with admirable poise, her family had welcomed Jason into the growing family with warm approval. They got along famously, as Madison did with Jason's close and demonstrative relatives.

Jason's parents, siblings, brother-in-law and nephews had traveled from Dallas to attend the wedding, and his Little Rock family was also in attendance. Madison watched Alice flirt with Justin D'Alessandro across the room, and then she laughed softly when Seth smoothly drew his daughter away to help Jacqui serve drinks. Seth had his hands full with his active teenage daughter; and he and Meagan had just learned the new baby was also a girl. Though Seth had wondered aloud if he would survive raising another daughter, there was no doubt to anyone who knew him that he was thrilled.

BiBi and Carl were there for the event, too. Madison couldn't have left BiBi out of the celebration, since it was at BiBi's wedding that this had all begun.

With her talent for rewriting her own personal

history, BiBi took full credit for the match. "I knew you and Jason would make a great couple," she said, giving Madison an enthusiastic hug.

Madison laughed, not bothering to point out that BiBi had tried to match her with another man altogether. "I'm so glad you could be here."

"I wouldn't have missed it for the world," BiBi assured. "Oh, and Corinna wanted me to give you and Jason hugs from her, too. She's very happy for you both, you know. She doesn't want any awkwardness in the future because of her silly crush on Jason. She and Brandon are really becoming an item these days. I wouldn't be surprised if they announce an engagement within the year."

"I'm glad she's happy."

"I'm glad we're *all* happy," BiBi agreed expansively. "And I can't wait until you move to Dallas. Aunt BiBi is going to spoil that baby of yours rotten, you know."

"I don't doubt it."

Jason joined them to hand Madison a flute of sparkling grape juice. "You two aren't plotting anything over here, by any chance, are you?"

Madison smiled at him over the rim of the glass. "Worried that I'm going to hit you with another big surprise?"

He grinned recklessly at her. "Bring it on. I can take it."

Laughing, she reached up to kiss his cheek. Her responsible family practitioner definitely had the soul of a fearless adventurer, she thought happily. Something told her that was going to come in quite handy during the busy, unpredictable and sometimes hectic life they would undoubtedly share.

Encouraged by the love that grew stronger with each passing day together, she had no doubt they were both up to the challenge.

* * * * *